Have yo[...]
FA[...]

(*Also available as dramatised recordings on CD)

A Note from Enid Blyton's Granddaughter

Welcome to the new edition of The Famous Five series by Enid Blyton. There are 21 books in the collection, a whole world of mystery and adventure to explore. My grandmother, Enid Blyton, wrote her first Famous Five Book, 'Five on a Treasure Island' in 1942. That was in the middle of World War Two (1939–1945). In the story, Julian, Dick and Anne meet their cousin Georgina and her dog, Timmy, for the first time. They soon learn *never* to call her Georgina. Together they explore tunnels and caves, discover hidden passageways and solve crimes.

I first met the Famous Five in a recording of 'Five have a Mystery to Solve'. Julian, Dick, George, Anne and Timmy have developed a love of sausages and can't seem to get enough of them. The sausages are put on hold when a lady knocks at the door of Kirrin Cottage. She has come to ask if the Five could keep her young grandson company in a remote cottage while she is away. The adventure begins as soon as they see the mysterious 'Whispering Island' as they cycle to the cottage to meet the grandson, Wilfred.

Timmy has always been my favourite character. He is the best judge of personality and when he is around, everything seems much safer; not that I am scared of adventure! Since watching the Famous Five television series in the 1970s, which cast Timmy as a Border-Collie sheep dog, I have always wanted to have a Border-Collie.

Who do you think you'll like best?

Sophie Smallwood, 14 June 2010

Short Story Collection

Enid Blyton

THE FAMOUS FIVE

Short Story Collection

Hodder
Children's
Books

A division of Hachette Children's Books

Typeset in Sabon by Avon DataSet Ltd, Bidford-on-Avon, Warwickshire

Printed and bound in Great Britain by Clays Ltd, St Ives plc

The paper and board used in this paperback by Hodder Children's Books
are natural recyclable products made from wood grown in sustainable
forests. The manufacturing processes conform to the environmental
regulations of the country of origin.

Hodder Children's Books
a division of Hachette Children's Books
338 Euston Road, London NW1 3BH
An Hachette UK company
www.hachette.co.uk

Contents

1 Five have a puzzling time

It was dark and very quiet in Kirrin Cottage – almost midnight. The Five were all in bed – yes, Timmy, the dog, too, for he was lying on George's feet, his usual place at night. He wasn't having a very comfortable time, because George, whose real name was Georgina, was so restless.

She tossed and turned and groaned – and at last awoke Anne, who was in the bed next to her.

'What's the matter, George?' said Anne, sleepily. 'Is your tooth aching again?'

'Yes, it's awful,' said George, sitting up with her hand to her cheek. 'Get off my feet, Timmy, I'll just *have* to get up and walk about!'

'Poor George,' said Anne. 'Good thing you're going to the dentist tomorrow!'

'Don't remind me of that!' said George, walking up and down the bedroom. 'Go to sleep, Anne – I didn't mean to disturb you.'

The big clock in the hall downstairs struck twelve, very slowly and solemnly. Anne listened, then her eyes shut and she fell asleep again. George went to the window and looked out over Kirrin Bay, holding a hand to her painful cheek. Timmy jumped off the bed and stood beside her, paws on the windowsill. He knew that George was in pain, and he was troubled. He rested his head against her hand and gave it a tiny lick.

'Dear Timmy,' said George. 'I hope *you'll* never have toothache! You'd go mad! Look at Kirrin Bay – isn't it lovely? And you can just see Kirrin Island – *my* island, Timmy – looming up in the darkness!'

Suddenly George stiffened and frowned. She stared across the bay, and then turned and called urgently to Anne.

'Anne! Quick, wake up! ANNE! Come and see! There's a light shining out on Kirrin Island, a light, I tell you! Somebody's there – on MY island! Anne, come and see!'

Anne sat up sleepily. 'What's the matter, George? What did you say?'

'I said there's a light on Kirrin Island! Somebody must be there – without permission too! I'll get my boat and row out right now!' George was very angry indeed, and Timmy gave a little growl. He would most certainly deal with whoever it was on the island!

'Oh, George – don't be an idiot!' said Anne. 'As if you could get your boat and row across the bay in the middle of the night! You must be mistaken!' She jumped out of bed and went to the window. 'Where's this light?'

'It's gone – it went out just as you jumped out of bed,' said George. 'Who can be there, Anne? I'll wake the boys and tell them. We'll get my boat.'

She went quickly down to the room where Dick and Julian lay asleep and shook them roughly.

'Wake up! Oh, PLEASE wake up! Something's going on over at Kirrin Island. I saw a light there. WAKE UP, Julian.'

George's excited voice not only woke up the boys, but her father as well. He sat up in bed in the next room, thinking there must be burglars in the house!

'Robbers, my dear!' he hissed in his wife's ear, making her start up in fright. 'Where's my big stick?'

'Quentin, it's only the children!' said his wife, sleepily. 'I expect George's toothache is worse. I'll go and see.'

Everybody met in the boys' room. 'What on earth is all this about?' demanded George's father.

'There's a light on Kirrin Island,' said George, quite fiercely. 'On *my* island! I'm going to see who it is – and so is Timmy. If no one will come with me I'll go alone.'

'Indeed you won't go,' said her father, raising his voice angrily. 'Get back to bed! Rowing to Kirrin Island in the middle of the night! You must be mad. There *can't* be anyone there. You've had a bad dream, or something.'

'Dad, there's a *light* there – I saw it!' said George, in a voice as loud as her father's. He went at once to the window and looked out.

'Rubbish!' he said. 'Not a glimmer of any sort to be seen! You dreamt it!'

'I did NOT!' said George, angrily. 'Somebody is there, I tell you. Trespassing!'

'Well, *let* them trespass!' said her father. 'You can go over tomorrow.'

'I *can't*!' almost wailed George. 'I've got to go

to the dentist, and have this nasty, horrible, awful tooth out. I *must* go tonight!'

'Shut up, George,' said Julian. 'Be sensible. Whoever's there will still be there tomorrow. I'll go over with Dick. Anyway, there's no light there now – you probably made a mistake. Go to bed, for goodness' sake.'

George flung out of the boys' room, and went to her own, furious. Timmy went with her, licking her now and again. Why couldn't he and George go off together, this very minute? Timmy was quite ready to!

'Now my tooth's aching worse than ever!' said poor George, angry and miserable, dumping herself violently on her bed. Her mother came over to her with a glass of water and two small pills.

'Take these, George,' she said. 'Your tooth will soon stop aching. Please be sensible, dear.'

'That's one thing George can't be!' said Anne, 'Cheer up, George – that tooth will be gone tomorrow – and there won't be anyone on your island, you'll see – and everything will be right again'.

George grunted, and lay down with her aching

cheek on her hand. She meant to slip out of bed, and go down to her boat as soon as the house was quiet again. But the little pills quickly did their work, and in five minutes her tooth had stopped aching, and she was fast asleep.

In the morning when she awoke, she remembered at once what she had seen the night before – a light on her island! And then she remembered the dentist – oh dear, two horrible thoughts – someone trespassing on her precious island – and a tooth to come out! She sat up in bed.

'Anne! My tooth has stopped aching. I won't go to the dentist, I'll go to Kirrin Island with Timmy and the boys.'

But her father thought differently, and after a really furious battle between the hot-tempered George and her equally hot-tempered father, George was packed off with her mother in the car, for her visit to the dentist! Timmy went with her, quite alarmed at all the goings-on!

'Poor George,' said Anne, as the car went off down the road. 'She does get so worked up about things.'

'Well, anyone gets upset with toothache,' said Julian. He stared out over Kirrin Bay, which was as blue as cornflowers that morning. 'I wonder if George *did* see a light on the island last night? *You* didn't see one, did you, Anne, when you awoke?'

'No. It was all dark there,' said Anne. 'Honestly, I think George must have dreamt it! Anyway she can take out her boat this afternoon, and we'll go with her, and have a good look round – that should satisfy her!'

'She may not feel like doing anything except having a bit of a rest,' said Dick. 'She's had toothache for days now, and it does get you down. I tell you what – we three will get the boat and go over to the island this morning – then, when we find nothing and nobody there – except the rabbits and the jackdaws – we can tell George, and she won't worry any more!'

'Right!' said Julian. 'Let's go now, straight away! Uncle Quentin will be glad to be rid of us – he's working hard this morning on one of his newest problems.'

George's father was glad to hear that the three were going off for the morning.

'Now I'll have the house to myself,' he said, thankfully. 'Except for Joanna, of course. I hope she doesn't take it into her head to clean out the boiler this morning – I MUST have peace and quiet.'

'You ought to invent a boiler that cleans *itself* out with hardly a whisper!' said Anne, smiling at her uncle. 'Anyway, we'll be out of your way. We're just going!'

They went to the beach, to get George's boat. There it was, ready waiting! Julian looked across to where Kirrin Island lay peacefully in the sun. He was quite certain there was nobody there! George must have dreamt the light she had seen shining in the night.

'We'll row right round the island and see if there's a boat tied up anywhere, or beached,' said Dick, taking the oars. 'If there isn't, we'll know there's no one there. It's too far for anyone to swim to. Well – here we go!'

And away they went in the warm spring sunshine, the little waves lapping cheerfully round the boat. Anne leaned back and let her hand dabble in the water – what fun to go over to the island and see all the rabbits – there would be young ones there too, now.

'Here we are, almost at the island,' said Julian.

'In and out of the rocks we go! I'm sorry for anyone who tries to come here in the middle of the night, unable to see what rocks to avoid! Not a sign of a boat anywhere – George *must* have dreamt it all!'

Dick rowed the boat carefully between the rocks that guarded the island.

'We'll land at our usual little cove,' he said. 'I bet no one else would know how to get there if they didn't already know the way!'

A low wall of sharp rocks came into sight and Dick rounded it neatly. Now they could see the cove where they meant to land – a little natural harbour, with a calm inlet of water running up to a smooth stretch of sand.

'The water's like glass here,' said Anne. 'I can see the bottom of the cove.' She leapt out and helped the boys to pull in the boat.

'*Look* at the rabbits!' said Dick, as they walked up the smooth sandy beach. 'Tame as ever!'

A small baby rabbit came lolloping up to Anne. 'You sweet little thing!' she said, trying to pick it up. 'You're just like a toy bunny!' But the tiny creature lolloped away again.

'Good thing Timmy's not here,' said Julian.

'He always looks so miserable when he sees the rabbits, because he knows he mustn't chase them!'

They came to the old ruined castle that had been built long ago on the island. The ancient, broken-down entrance led into a great yard, overgrown with weeds. Now the jackdaws came down from the tower, and chacked loudly round them in a very friendly manner. Some of them flew down to the children's feet, and walked about as tame as hens in a farm yard.

'Well – it doesn't look as if anyone's here,' said Julian, staring round and about.

'And there was no boat anywhere,' said Anne. 'So how could anyone have come here? Let's see if there are any signs of a fire having been lighted. The flames would be seen at night, if so.'

They began to hunt all around. They went in and out of the old castle, examining the floor – but there was no sign of anyone having made a fire.

'If George saw a light, then there must be a lamp or lantern somewhere,' said Dick. 'Anne, did she see the light high up on the island – as if it came from the tower?'

'She didn't say,' said Anne. 'But I should *think* it must have been high up. We'll go up the old broken-down tower steps as far as we can, shall we? We might see something there – perhaps a lantern. It's possible, I suppose, that someone might have been signalling for some reason!'

But, no matter how they searched, the three could find nothing to explain the light that George had said she saw.

'Let's go and lie down on the grass, and watch the rabbits,' said Anne. 'Hey – why did the jackdaws all fly up then – and why are they chacking so much? What frightened them?'

'Funny!' said Julian, staring at the big black birds, circling round and round above them, calling 'chack-chack-chack' so excitedly. '*We* didn't scare them, I'm sure. I suppose there *can't* be someone else here?'

'Well – we'll walk round the island and examine the rocks sticking up here and there,' said Dick, puzzled about the jackdaws, too. 'Someone might be hiding behind one of them.'

'I'm going to take off my sandals,' said Anne. 'I love running on the smooth sand in bare feet. I'll have a paddle, too – the water's quite warm today!'

The boys wandered off round the island. Anne sat down and undid her sandals. She set them by a big stone, so that she could easily find them again, and ran down to the sea. Little waves were splashing over the smooth golden sand, and Anne ran into them, curling up her toes in pleasure.

'It's really almost warm enough to swim,' she thought. 'What a lovely little island this is – and how lucky George is to own it. I wish *I* had an island belonging to my family, that I could call my own. If I had, I suppose I'd worry, too, like George, if I thought anyone was trespassing here – scaring the rabbits – and even perhaps snaring them!'

Soon Julian and Dick came back together, having gone all round the island, and looked into every cranny. They called to Anne.

'Hello, paddler! Is the water nice and warm? We should have brought our swimming things.'

'We haven't seen a sign of a single soul,' said Dick. 'Better go home again. George may be back by now – wanting to tell us about her tooth, and what she's been through. Poor George!'

'I'll put on my sandals,' said Anne, drying her feet by scrabbling them in the warm sand. She ran to the big stone by which she had put them. She stopped – and stared in surprise.

'What's happened to one of my sandals? Dick – Ju – have you taken one? Where have you put it?'

'Sandals? No – we didn't even know where you'd put them,' said Julian. 'There's one of them there, look – the other must be somewhere near.'

But it wasn't. No matter how they all looked, only one of Anne's sandals could be found!

'*Well*! How silly!' said Anne, amazed. 'I *know* I put them both together, just here. I know I did! Anyway, there's no one to take one of my sandals – and even if there were, why take one, and not both?'

'Perhaps a rabbit took one?' suggested Dick, with a grin. 'Or a jackdaw – they're really mischievous birds, you know!'

'A jackdaw surely couldn't pick up a *sandal*!' said Anne. 'It'd be too heavy. And I can't *imagine* a rabbit running off with one!'

'Well – it's not there,' said Dick, thinking to himself that Anne must have been mistaken about putting them both by the big stone. He hunted round, but could not see the other one anywhere – strange! However – there certainly was no one on the island – and, if there had been, someone wouldn't have been so silly as to risk being discovered by stealing one little sandal, in full view of Anne!

'We'll have to leave your sandal, wherever it is, Anne,' said Julian, at last. 'We ought to get back. Well – the only thing we can tell George is that we saw no one at all here – but that one sandal mysteriously disappeared!'

'Oh no!' said Anne, not bothering to put on her one sandal. 'Now I'll have to spend some of my precious pocket money to buy a pair of new sandals. How annoying!'

'Come on,' said Dick, going down towards their boat. 'George'll have a fit if we don't turn up soon. She'll think that the owner of the mysterious light has caught us and made us prisoners! Hurry up, Anne.'

They were soon all in the boat again, and the boys took it in turn to row back. Through the crowd of rocks they went, threading their way carefully, and at last came to their own beach.

George was there, waiting for them, Timmy beside her!

'You went without me!' she scolded. 'You really are horrible! What did you find?'

'Nothing and no one. The island's absolutely empty except for its usual inhabitants – rabbits and jackdaws!' said Julian, dragging the boat up the sand. 'Your strange light in the night must have been a dream, George!'

'It was NOT!' said George, and her voice was so angry that Timmy began to bark. 'You don't know where to look! Now if Timmy had been with you, he'd have smelt out anyone there – he'd have found the lamp or lantern – he'd have . . .'

'All right, all right – but we didn't *have* Timmy!' said Dick.

'How's the tooth, George?' said Anne, seeing that George's cheek was still swollen. 'Did you have it out? Did it hurt?'

But George didn't want to waste time in talking about her tooth.

'It's out,' she said, shortly. 'Horrible tooth! If I hadn't had to go to the dentist, I could have gone with you – and I BET Timmy and I would have found something. I just BET we would!'

'All right – go there, then – and take Tim with you,' said Dick, exasperated.

'That's just what I *will* do!' said George with a scowl. '*We'll* soon find out who's hiding there. I'll go this afternoon – with Timmy. You can come, too, if you like, of course – but I can't see that you'll be much use!'

'Oh, we'll come all right!' said Dick. 'Even if it's only to say, "Told you so" when you can't find more than *we* did!'

George had made up her mind to go off in her boat after she had had her dinner.

'Although my mouth is so sore I'm sure I won't be able to eat anything!' she said. However, she ate as much as any of the others! Timmy sat very close to her, sad that she was cross and upset.

It wasn't a very happy meal. Uncle Quentin was quiet and moody, for his work hadn't gone well that morning. Aunt Fanny looked worried. George sulked. Timmy kept giving heavy sighs.

Even Joanna the cook added a few cross words as she cleared away the dinner.

'I'd like to know who's been at the grapes and the oranges,' she said. '*Someone* came downstairs in the night and helped themselves. And George – what did you do with the bag of dog biscuits that came from the grocer's yesterday? I couldn't find any for Tim's dinner.'

'Oh don't fuss, Joanna!' said George. 'You know where I always put them – in the outhouse, with the chicken food.'

'Well, you didn't this time,' said Joanna, huffily.

'You can't have *looked*,' said George. 'Oh dear – why do all these things have to happen when I've a bad tooth?'

'Well – you certainly *shouldn't* have a bad tooth now,' remarked Julian. 'I thought the dentist . . .'

'All right, all right – yes, he *did* pull it out, but it still feels as if it's there,' said George, crossly.

'You'd better have a lie down this afternoon, George,' said her mother. 'A little sleep will . . .'

'Put you right!' chorused Julian, Dick and Anne, who had heard this saying of their aunt's a hundred times.

She laughed. 'Well – what with toothache all night, and little sleep, it's no wonder poor George is cross.'

'I'm NOT cross!' roared George, furiously, and that made everyone laugh, of course. Julian gave her a pat on the back.

'Cheer up. We'll all go and hunt over the island again this afternoon – and I expect you'll find a couple of pirates, two or three robbers, a shipwrecked sailor, a . . .'

George gave a sudden grin. 'Shut up, you idiot. Don't take any notice of me for a bit. I'll be all right soon.'

And she was. She took herself in hand, helped Joanna with the washing up, and then went to look for the biscuits for Timmy. Sure enough, they were missing, as Joanna had said.

'I'm *sure* I put them in the outhouse here,' said George, looking all around. 'I suppose I couldn't have. What *have* I done with them? Poor Tim – you'll have to make do with scraps, I'm afraid, till the butcher boy comes with your meat this afternoon. And by the way, Joanna, I did NOT come down last night and take grapes and oranges. My tooth was much too bad. And *I'd* like to know something now. Who's been at my big box of chocolates?'

She had opened a large box, and was staring

inside. 'There's more than half gone!' she said. 'Timmy – have you been at them? Were you so hungry, poor thing?'

'Well, I must say that if he took them he was clever to put back the lid!' said Joanna. 'Maybe you ate an orange or two as well, Timmy-dog?'

'Woof,' said Timmy, in disgust, and turned his back on Joanna. As if he would steal chocolates or oranges!

George went off to find her mother. 'Mum – I feel better now. The swelling in my mouth is going down at top speed. I'll be all right to take the boat out with the others, really I will.'

'Well – your dad does want peace and quiet this afternoon,' said her mother. 'Go along, then – and don't get over-tired – you had quite a bad time this morning.'

Within ten minutes all the Five were in the boat once more. George was her old self again, and Julian grinned at her.

'Well? All set to find what we couldn't find? I must admit that with Timmy to help us, we're much more likely to be successful!'

They soon came to the island. George circled it deftly in the boat, being anxious herself to see that no one had hidden a boat anywhere. She pointed to where a great mass of brown seaweed had piled up on the west shore.

'See what the wind did when we had that terrific gale on Tuesday – brought in masses of seaweed again! Now we'll have an awful smell when it dries out! Hey – what's wrong with the jackdaws, all of a sudden? They're never scared of *us*! Why are they flying up in such a hurry? There *is* someone on the island!'

That's what *we* thought this morning,' said Dick, with a grin. 'But there wasn't! Plenty of rabbits, though – hundreds. Thank goodness there's *one* place left where they can live in peace!'

George swung the boat round and ran it deftly into the little cove. Out they all leapt, and pulled in the boat. Timmy jumped out first and tore up the beach at full speed, barking.

'That'll scare the life out of anyone hiding!' said George, pleased. 'Go on, Tim – bark. Hunt around! Sniff everywhere!'

The rabbits scattered at once when they heard Timmy. 'Don't you dare to touch them!' George called to him, knowing how much he longed to catch one. 'Heel, now, Timmy, heel! I want you to come round every corner of the island with me.'

Timmy ran to heel, his long tail swinging happily. He loved Kirrin Island. George set off, meaning to examine every well-loved corner, every possible hiding place. They came to a group of bushes and Timmy began to sniff about at once.

'He can smell something there!' said George, excited. 'What is it, Tim?'

But apparently he found nothing of interest, and soon joined them again. Then Anne's sharp eyes caught sight of something bright under a bush and she bent down to see what it was. She looked round at the others, astonished.

'Look – orange peel! Someone *must* have been here then! We'd never leave orange peel about! And look, what's *this*!'

They all clustered round and looked where Anne was pointing. George bent down and picked up something very small.

'See – a pip – a pip from a grape. Does that ring a bell, anyone?'

'Yes!' said Dick. 'Joanna said we'd been at the oranges and grapes – do you think that . . .'

'No! Who's going to steal a bit of fruit and take it over to the island to eat!' said Julian. 'That's too far-fetched, honestly! Let's be sensible!'

'What's Timmy doing?' said Anne, suddenly. 'Hey, Tim – don't scrape all the sand off the island!'

Timmy was feverishly scraping at the sand nearby with his front paws. He gave an excited little bark, that sounded pleased. What on earth had he found? The others ran to him at once.

Timmy had made a hole – and in it something showed – it seemed like a bulky bag of some kind. Timmy took hold of it with his teeth, and pulled. It split at once – and to everyone's enormous astonishment, out came a mass of dog biscuits!

How they stared! DOG biscuits! Surely, surely they couldn't be the biscuits that George had bought for Timmy the day before, and put in the outhouse?

'They *are*!' said George. 'Look – exactly the same kind. Isn't this strange! Who on earth would want to steal dog biscuits and bring them here – and oranges and grapes – and for goodness' sake, WHY?'

Nobody could think of an answer. Timmy began to crunch up the biscuits, looking very pleased indeed with himself. He didn't know who had buried them on Kirrin Island, but he thought it was a very good idea!

'Well, that settles it,' said Julian. 'You were right, George – someone is here – and you *did* see a light on the island in the middle of the night. But how did they get here without a boat?'

'We'll soon find out!' said George grimly. 'We know he's a thief, anyway! Tim – go to it! Find him, find him, whoever he is! Smell him out, Tim, smell him out!'

And off went Tim at once, nose to the ground, following the scent of the thief – now WHERE would he lead them? And whoever would he find? It really was too exciting for words.

Timmy went off at such a speed that the four couldn't keep up with him. He raced off round the castle, nose to ground, barking loudly.

'He'll certainly warn anyone in hiding that he's on their track,' panted Dick. 'Where on earth can they be? We've hunted everywhere!'

Over the sand and on to the rocks went Timmy, right up to where the seaweed was piled in great masses by the wind and the waves. He stopped and began to sniff anxiously.

'He's lost the trail!' said George, disappointed. 'It's the smell of the seaweed that's put him off.'

'Or else whoever was here came in a boat at high tide, which would bring it to the shore – and has sailed off again now the tide has gone out,' said Julian, frowning. 'There wouldn't be any trail to smell, then. Honestly, there doesn't seem to be *anyone* hiding – and now that even Tim is stumped, I think we're too late to find whoever it was.'

'Timmy – sniff round again,' said George. 'Go on – you may pick up some other trail.'

Timmy obediently sniffed here and there, and occasionally gave a strange growl of anger. Why? George was puzzled.

'Why does he sound so fierce?' she said. 'Really angry! What is it, Timmy?'

'Perhaps he doesn't like the smell of whoever has been here,' said Anne. 'Let's sit down for a bit and watch the rabbits and the jackdaws. Ju, did you bring any biscuits? I brought some barley sugars, and Dick's brought some chocolate in his pocket – I hope it won't be melted!'

George wanted to go on hunting, but the others felt that it was no use. If Timmy had found the scent, and couldn't follow it, no one else would be able to! Anyway, probably the trespasser was far away by now, safely in his boat!

Anne chose a sunny corner by an old ruined wall, and they sat down. At first the rabbits kept away from the children and Timmy – but soon they came out again, as tame as ever. The jackdaws came down too, running almost up to the children, hoping for a titbit.

Suddenly one jackdaw ran at a baby rabbit and gave it a hard peck in the back of the neck. The tiny thing fell over dazed, and all the jackdaws came round it in excitement.

'Oh, they'll *all* peck it now!' cried Anne, jumping up. 'Shoo, you birds!'

The birds flew off, chacking loudly, and the little rabbit began to crawl away, still dazed. It tried to run when the children went after it to pick it up, and disappeared under a bush.

'We'll have to get it out to make sure it's not *really* hurt,' said Anne, anxiously. So the boys crawled under the bush, trying to find where the tiny creature had hidden itself. As it was a gorse bush it was very prickly, and Dick groaned.

'I'm being torn to pieces by these thorns. The rabbit's gone, Anne. I think it's found a rabbit hole and gone down it. I expect its mother's down there. She'll lick it better.'

They went back to where they had left their biscuits and bars of chocolate. Anne stopped suddenly and stared down in amazement.

'Look! Half the biscuits have gone – and two of the chocolate bars! Surely the jackdaws couldn't have taken them so quickly!'

'There's a broken biscuit over here, look – it must have been dropped by whoever stole them!' said Dick, amazed. 'What a nerve to come right up to where we were sitting, and take the things just when our backs were turned. I didn't hear a thing!'

'Nor did Tim – or he would have barked,' said George, really puzzled. 'Whoever it was must have come up as quietly as a mouse!'

'Let Timmy sniff round – he'll pick up the trail,' said Julian. 'It'll be so fresh!' Timmy was already sniffing, looking very puzzled indeed. The trail didn't seem much use to him! He ran a little way, nose to ground, following it – and then stopped, as if the trail had come to an end!

'Look, Timmy – trails don't finish all of a sudden!' said George, exasperated. 'People don't take off in mid-air!'

'There's a tree nearby,' said Anne. 'Do you think whoever it was could have climbed up into it?'

'Anne, there's NOBODY up the tree,' said George, in a patient, what-an-idiot-you-are sort of voice. 'I've looked.'

'Well, let's hunt round a bit again,' said Julian, more puzzled than ever. 'I know – we'll leave some biscuits and the bag of barley sugars here, and go behind that big gorse bush and hide – and maybe the thief, whoever he is, will come along and take *those*. He seems to have a sweet tooth!'

'Good idea,' said Dick. 'Come on, everyone – you too, Timmy – and not a sound from anyone, mind!'

'They went behind the gorse bush and waited. Dick peeped out once or twice, but the bag of barley sugars remained untouched. Then suddenly Timmy gave a low growl, leapt out from behind the gorse bush and ran at something! Everyone followed in excitement. Who was it?

There was nobody there! But up on one of the branches of the nearby tree sat the thief, a barley sugar clutched in his hand, chattering angrily.

'It's a monkey – a little *monkey*!' cried George, in the greatest astonishment. 'It was *he* who took the other things! Wherever did he come from?'

The monkey leapt to the top of a broken wall, chattered again at them, and disappeared. Timmy raced to the wall, but the monkey was nowhere to be seen.

'Well – what do you think of *that*?' said Dick. 'A monkey! Where has he come from? *Some*body must have brought him here – but why? And is that somebody still here – or has he gone?'

'I bet it was that monkey who came and stole my sandal this morning!' said Anne, suddenly.

'Of course!' said Julian. 'This *is* a puzzle! What do we do next?'

'Well, there's one thing we *do* know – and that is that a monkey wouldn't light a fire or a lamp at night on the island,' said Dick. 'That must have been done by a human being – and he MUST still be on the island if his monkey's here.

He surely wouldn't go away and leave the little thing to starve.'

'Oh, *no* – it's such a sweet little creature,' said Anne. 'It had a really comical little face – did you notice? Thank goodness it left us most of the barley sugars. Let's have some, before anything else happens!'

They sat sucking the barley sugars, really puzzled. 'Buried dog biscuits!' said Julian. 'A monkey that steals food – and sandals! By the way, let's go and have a look at where we left those dog biscuits – maybe they've gone as well!'

They went off to see – but no, there were the scattered biscuits. Timmy helped himself to a few again, and a loud crunching filled the air. The jackdaws hopped near, hoping to pick up a few crumbs. Timmy ran at them, and then stopped and put his nose down to the ground. He had picked up the same scent as before!

'Follow the trail again, Tim,' said Julian. 'You may do better this time. Go on!'

But before Timmy could even put his head down again to follow it, something odd happened. A strange noise came from the west side of the island – the miserable howling of a dog!

'That's a *dog*!' cried Dick, amazed. 'On the island, too – whatever next! Where is he?'

'Oh, quick – he sounds as if he's in trouble!' cried George. 'What's happening? Quick, Julian, quick, Timmy! Oh, poor thing, there he goes, howling again. We *must* find him, we must!'

The Five set off in the direction of the howls, Timmy racing ahead anxiously. He knew far better than the others that a dog was in sore trouble – a howling of that kind meant not only pain, but terror. But how did a dog come to be on the island – and a monkey, too! Timmy was as puzzled as the children.

Julian was now in front of the other three, and was heading for the seaweed-spread shore on the west of the island. George suddenly gave a cry, and pointed.

'There's the monkey again! He's seen us – he's racing away!'

'Maybe he'll lead us to wherever the dog is,' shouted Julian. The monkey scampered in front, just ahead of Timmy. They all came to the shore, and stopped when they came to the piled-up heaps of brown, slippery seaweed, covering the rocks in great masses.

'The dog's stopped howling,' said George, looking all round. 'I'm sure he must be *some*where near here. What's the monkey doing? Look – he's running out over the seaweed. He'll slip into a pool and drown!'

They watched the tiny brown monkey. He was making his way over the seaweed-covered rocks now, avoiding the pools of water here and there. Further and further out he went. George started to go, too, but Julian pulled her back.

'No. That seaweed is slippery – it's too dangerous to go out on those rocks – we know the sea is very deep in between. *Look* at that little monkey – where on earth does he think he's going?'

The monkey came to a rock that was absolutely covered with thick masses of seaweed flung there by the surging, wind-blown tide. He had no sooner arrived there than an extraordinary thing happened!

A small mass of seaweed moved – and out of it came something that made the Five stare in utter disbelief.

'It can't be!' muttered Dick. 'No – it *can't* be!'

It was the brown and white head of a big dog!

The Five stared, unable to move. Never had they expected to see such a thing! The head suddenly opened a great mouth and howled dismally! In a flash, Timmy was over the seaweed-y rocks, barking for all he was worth as if to say, 'Hold on, friend, I'm coming!'

And then another surprising thing happened! A second head poked up from under a covering of seaweed, and a voice shouted loudly, 'Tell your dog to keep off! Mine will fight him! And go away, all of you!'

The Five were so full of amazement that they stood like statues, unable to say a word. Then George, afraid that the hidden dog might attack Timmy, yelled to him.

'Tim! Come back! Tim, do you hear me? Heel, Tim, heel!'

Timmy turned, and came back very sulkily, his tail down. *Why* had George called him back at such an exciting moment? He had only wanted to help the other dog!

The second head was still poking out of its strange seaweed-y hiding place – the head of a small boy! Julian really could not believe his eyes. So *that* was the hiding place – under the seaweed – and the dog was there, too – and probably the monkey had hidden there as well! What *was* going on?

'Hey, you there in the seaweed – come on out!' yelled Julian. 'We won't hurt you. If you want help, we'll give it to you. Come on out, and tell us what you're doing!'

'All right. But if you try to catch me, I'll set my dog on you!' yelled back a defiant voice. 'He's a cross-bred Alsatian and he could eat up your dog in one gulp!'

'We won't do anything to hurt you or your dog,' yelled back Dick. 'We heard him howling, poor thing. He's terrified of being under the seaweed. COME ON OUT!'

And then the seaweed pile was heaved up and down, and out came a scraggy, wet boy of about eleven. He pulled the seaweed off the dog, who was quite weighted down by it. The great animal shook itself, and gave one more miserable howl.

'You look out for your dog!' yelled the boy. 'Mine's fierce. There'll be a terrible fight if yours goes for mine.'

But Timmy had no idea of fighting such a wet, miserable and hungry dog! He waited until the boy and the Alsatian came scrambling towards the Five, over the rocks, and then he leapt lightly over the seaweed, and ran to the great Alsatian, his long tail wagging in welcome. He whined a little to him, and then licked his face, as if to say, 'Cheer up! I'm your friend!'

The Alsatian gave a little growl – and then an apologetic bark. He wagged his wet tail, and then, side by side with Timmy, ran up the shore to the waiting children.

The boy came scrambling along next, the little monkey now chattering on his shoulder, holding on to the boy's hair to save himself from falling. The Five were almost too astonished to say a word, but the two dogs made up for their silence by racing along the beach, barking madly.

The boy looked half scared, half sulky, and stared at them defiantly. George spoke to him first.

'What are you doing on my island?'

'Nothing,' said the boy. 'I just came here – with my dog and monkey – for – well – for a little holiday.'

'How did you come here?' asked Julian. 'We didn't see any boat.'

'I didn't *come* in a boat,' said the boy.

'Well, what *did* you come in, then?' asked Dick, astonished.

'I won't tell you,' said the boy. 'If I did you'd take it away from me – and, and . . .'

And then, to the dismay of the Five he began to cry bitterly, tears pouring down his cheeks. The little monkey put his arms round the boy's neck and loved him, and the dog leapt up, licking him wherever he could, whining in sympathy.

'Oh, don't cry like that!' said Anne, horrified. She took the boy's hand and led him along the beach. 'It's all right. We're your friends. We like your monkey and your dog. Tell us what's the matter. We'll help you!'

Soon they were all sitting down, the monkey still on the boy's shoulder, the dog close beside him. Even Timmy sat as close to the boy as he could, upset because of his tears.

'Have a barley sugar?' said Dick. 'Take two. That's right. Now, tell us what's been happening? Why did you come here – and how?'

'There's not much to tell,' said the boy. 'My name's Bobby Loman. I live with my Granpop in Kirrin Village. My mum and dad are dead, and

I'm on my own – except for Chippy the monkey here, and Chummy, my Alsatian. I've run away. That's all.'

'No,' said Anne gently. 'That isn't all. Tell us *everything*, Bobby.'

'Oh, well – it's not much,' said Bobby. 'Granpop hates Chippy, my monkey, because he steals things. And Chummy costs a lot to keep – and – and – you see, he bit someone last week – and Granpop said he was to be put to sleep. Chummy, killed. He's my best friend! There's nobody he loves better than me, you don't know how kind and good he is, he sleeps on my bed at night, he licks me when things are bad, he – he . . .'

Bobby began to cry again, and the Alsatian nestled close to him and licked his cheek.

'See what I mean?' said Bobby. 'He loves me! He's the only person who does – and I WON'T have him put to sleep. Well – would you have this nice dog of *yours* killed?'

'NO! Never, never, NEVER!' said George, and put her arms round a surprised Timmy. 'You're quite right to run away, Bobby. I'm GLAD you came to my island. VERY glad. You and Chippy and Chummy can live here as long as you like.

We'll bring you food each day, we'll . . .'

'Hold on, George,' said Julian. 'Don't make promises we can't keep. Let's go back to Kirrin Cottage and tell your mum about this – she'll know what's best to do. Bobby can stay with us, perhaps, till things are settled.'

'Oh – what fun to have another dog *and* a monkey, as well as Timmy,' said Anne. 'Bobby – how did you come to the island, if you didn't have a boat?'

'Oh – that was easy,' said Bobby. 'I've got one of those blow up beds. Chippy and I sailed on it, with a spade for an oar – and Chummy swam alongside. It's buried in the sand, so that nobody would see it. But I didn't have any food, so . . .'

'So you crept into our outhouse last night and took a bag of dog biscuits for Chummy, and some fruit for Chippy,' said Julian. 'What about yourself?'

'Oh – I've been eating the dog biscuits,' said Bobby. 'I took some chocolates too, and ate those. I'm sorry about the stealing. I was sort of – sort of – desperate, you know. I'll pay back for everything I took.'

'Come on – let's get back home,' said Julian,

see.ng that Bobby was tired out, cold, wet, and probably very hungry. Come along now – we'll get our boat!'

The Five went back to where they had left George's boat, and took Bobby, Chippy, the monkey and Chummy the Alsatian with them. Timmy was very kind to them all, and wagged his tail hard the whole time, to show how friendly he was.

'I'm a bit scared of seeing your mum and dad,' said Bobby, in the boat. 'You're sure they won't send me off to a children's home – or to prison, or something like that? Chummy here would fret like anything if I went away from him.'

'I don't think you need worry,' said Julian, who was rowing. 'And I wouldn't be surprised if your Granpop was very pleased to hear you're safe.'

Bobby looked doubtful, but said no more. He cuddled up to Timmy and Chummy, who both took turns at licking him. Chippy the monkey was very lively and leapt from one person to another, making a funny little chattering noise. He took Dick's handkerchief out of his pocket and pretended to blow his nose on it.

'Hey – you're not to take things from people, I've told you that before!' said Bobby. 'Ooooh – that reminds me – he brought this shoe to me this morning – does it belong to any of you?'

And out of his pocket he took – one red sandal! Anne gave a delighted yell.

'OH! It's mine. I missed it this morning. Oh *good* – now I won't have to buy a new pair! Chippy – you really are a monkey!'

'There's no doubt about *that*!' said Dick grinning, and Chippy made his chattering noise as if he understood every word!

George's mother was very astonished to see a monkey, a dog and another boy added to the Five when they arrived at Kirrin Cottage.

'Who are all these?' she said. 'I don't mind the dog, George, but I will *not* have a monkey running loose in the house.'

'He can sleep in the shed, Mum,' said George. 'Please don't say he can't. Mum, this is Bobby – he ran away from his grandfather who wanted to put his lovely dog to sleep.'

'Bobby? Bobby Loman do you mean?' said Mrs Kirrin at once. 'He was in the papers today – and a picture of the dog and the monkey too! Bobby, your grandfather is very unhappy and worried. You were a silly little boy to run away just because of an upset. I'm *sure* your grandfather would never have had your dog destroyed. He only said that in the heat of the moment – when he was very cross!'

Bobby looked rather scared at Mrs Kirrin's forthright words. George put her arm around his shoulder.

'Mum!' she said, 'I'm sure *I'd* run away if you threatened to do anything to Timmy – so I do understand why Bobby ran away to my island. Well – *sailed* away!'

'Oh – so *that's* who it was on your island last night!' said Mrs Kirrin. 'Well, well, well! You Five do seem to run into adventure, don't you? How did he get there? And what was the light you saw?'

'I floated there on my air bed,' said Bobby. 'Oh – I've forgotten it! It's still on the island. The light George saw was my torch, I expect. I was looking for somewhere safe to sleep. I never imagined anyone would see the light of a torch in the dark of midnight!'

'Oh, you don't know George!' said Dick. 'If

anyone happened to strike even a match on her beloved island, she'd be sure to be looking out of the window at that very moment, and see the flare. Then we'd all have to go rushing off to find out what it was.'

'Shut up,' said George, crossly. 'It's a good thing I did look out of the window last night – if I hadn't, goodness knows what would have happened to Bobby and the monkey and Chummy – they might have starved to death.'

'Well, we still had plenty of dog biscuits left,' said Bobby. 'They weren't bad – but very hard. I got Chummy to bite them in half for me.'

'How very disgusting!' said Mrs Kirrin. 'Now let's think what's best to do. What's your grandfather's phone number, Bobby? I'll ring him up at once, and then you can go home. I hope you'll tell him you're sorry for being such a silly boy!'

'Er, Mum – I've asked Bobby to stay the night,' said George. 'Mum, the monkey's so sweet. You'll love him. And Chummy is wonderful. You should have seen him with Timmy – they were like old friends at once.'

'Very well. Bobby can stay the night,' said

George's mother, and Bobby beamed all over his face.

'If I had a tail I'd wag it hard,' he said, and that made everyone laugh.

Things were soon settled. Mrs Kirrin rang up the police to tell them Bobby was safe. Then she rang up his grandfather and told him the news too. The old man was so relieved that he could hardly thank Mrs Kirrin enough.

'I *wouldn't* have had his dog put to sleep,' he said. 'I just said that to make Bobby more careful with Chummy. Now that the dog's growing so big and strong, he must be properly trained, and must never bite anyone – Bobby's too easy with him. I'll send the dog to a trainer, and when he comes back he'll be quite all right, and Bobby can have him again.'

Bobby didn't think much of this idea when Mrs Kirrin told him.

'I just *won't* let Chummy go to a cruel trainer!' he said, looking round at the others for sympathy. But even George rounded on him at once.

'There! You care more for your own feelings than for Chummy's well-being! Don't you *want* a dog who's safe even with a small child? Don't you *want* a dog who'll obey you at once, and be a credit to you – like Timmy is to me?'

'All right, all right. Don't bite my head off. Sounds as if *you* ought to go to a trainer too!' said Bobby. 'Going round snapping at people!'

'Mum! I don't want Bobby to stay the night after all!' said George, fiercely.

'Oh *look* at that monkey – he's taken a banana from the dish, and he's peeling it just like a human being!' cried Anne, changing the subject very neatly indeed. 'Aunt Fanny, look – isn't he sweet?'

In the end Bobby was allowed to stay the night, and slept downstairs in the kitchen on a sofa, with Chippy cuddled beside him, and Chummy on his feet. Upstairs George was in bed with Timmy on *her* feet, talking about the excitements of the day with Anne.

'How's your tooth?' asked Anne, suddenly remembering the night before, when George had had such bad toothache, and had wandered about the bedroom, and seen a light on Kirrin Island.

'Tooth? What tooth?' said George, surprised. She had forgotten all about it in the excitement of the afternoon. 'Oh, the one I had out. Doesn't it seem AGES since this morning!'

She put her tongue into the space where the tooth had been. 'I think a new one's growing already,' she said. 'I wish I had teeth like Timmy – snowy white – strong – fierce. I'd like to be able to show all my teeth like Timmy, when I feel really angry!'

Anne laughed. 'Well – you *almost* manage it now,' she said. 'Hey – what's the matter with Timmy? He's pretty restless tonight. Look – he's gone to the door. He wants to go out.'

'All he wants is to go and have a talk to Chummy,' said George. 'All right, Tim. You can go down to the kitchen and sleep with Chummy if you like. I suppose you think he might be lonely. I bet he was scared when he had to hide under that wet, smelly seaweed!'

Timmy pattered down the stairs as soon as the bedroom door was opened. He scraped at the kitchen door and Bobby got up to open it. He was surprised and pleased to see Timmy, who licked him lavishly, and then went to lie beside the pleased Alsatian. It wasn't often that Timmy had a doggy visitor and he meant to make the most of it!

George took one more look out of the window before she got into bed – and gave a sudden exclamation.

'Anne – I think there's a light on Kirrin Island again. Anne – come and look!'

'Don't be an idiot,' said Anne, sleepily. 'You don't think we're going to start this adventure all over again, do you? It's FINISHED, George, not just beginning. Come back to bed.'

George jumped into bed. 'It *was* a light,' she said, after a moment or two. 'But only a shooting star! What a pity! I'd have liked another adventure – wouldn't you, Anne?'

But Anne was fast asleep, dreaming of monkeys, red sandals, seaweed, big dogs and orange peel. Well – I'm not really surprised at that – are you?

2 George's hair is too long

'Let's go to Windy Cove,' said Julian one fine summer's day in August. 'It's so hot on Kirrin Beach – Windy Cove will be nice and cool. There's always a breeze blowing there.'

'Right,' said Dick. 'What do you say, George?'

'Well, I wanted to go and have my hair cut,' said George. 'Honestly, it'll be as long as Anne's if I don't have it cut soon.'

'Well, I wish you *would* have it cut,' said Dick. 'You keep on complaining about it – as if it mattered whether it was short or long.'

'You forget that it matters to George very much,' said Julian with a grin. 'People *might* mistake her for a girl if it grows half an inch longer! Well, for goodness' sake, George, get it cut this afternoon. We pass the hairdresser's on the way to Windy Cove. We'll all go into the dairy and have ice-creams, and wait for you there.'

They set off at two o'clock. The road to the

village was hot and dusty, and Timmy ran along with his long pink tongue hanging halfway down his front legs!

'Poor Tim – you can have an ice-cream, too,' said Dick, patting him.

They came to the village, and George went to the hairdresser's shop while the others went on with Timmy to the dairy, which sold good creamy ice-creams. They heard George calling them and turned.

'The shop's shut! It's early-closing day,' she shouted. 'I forgot. Now I can't have my hair cut.'

'Well, never mind – come and have an ice-cream,' shouted back Julian. But George was in an obstinate mood.

'No. I want my hair cut, even if I have to cut it myself! Anybody got a pair of scissors?'

'Of course not. Who carries scissors about? Don't be an idiot!' said Dick. 'For goodness' sake come on with us and stop worrying about your hair.'

'I'll go and borrow some scissors in the ironmonger's,' shouted George. 'They're shut, too, but I know old Mr Pails will let me in at the side door. You go on with Timmy and have ice-creams. I don't want one. I'll catch you up when I'm ready.'

'What an idiot George is,' said Dick, going on with the others. 'Once she's made up her mind to do something, nothing will stop her, not even if it doesn't really matter.'

They went to the dairy. George went round to the side door of the ironmonger's shop. Mr Pails answered her knock.

'Well, George, what do you want?' he said. 'My shop's shut, as you very well know, and I'm just going to catch the bus over to my son's, as I always do on early-closing day.'

'I won't keep you more than a minute,' said George. 'I want to borrow a pair of nice sharp scissors, Mr Pails. Only just for a minute or two. The bus doesn't go for ten minutes; you've got plenty of time.'

'Well, well, you always were a one for getting your own way!' said the old man. 'Come on in – I'll show you the drawer where the scissors are kept. But don't you be long now – I must catch that bus!'

George went down the passage that led to the

shop and the old man took her to a drawer at the back. He was just opening it when a small van drew up outside the shop. It stopped and two men got out. George looked up casually – and jumped! One of the men was peering through the letterbox on the shop door. What an extraordinary thing to do!

George distinctly saw the man's eyes looking through the letterbox into the dark shop. She pulled at Mr Pail's arm and whispered.

'Do you see that man peering through the letterbox? What does he want? He couldn't have seen us because we're in such a dark corner.'

At that very moment the door was forced open and two men came hurriedly into the shop. At first they didn't see Mr Pails and George, and made for the little black safe set at the back of the counter. Mr Pails gave an indignant shout.

'Hey, you! What do you mean, forcing your way in here? I'll . . .'

But one of the men leapt over to him and put his hand over the old man's mouth. The other man ran to George and swung her into a little cupboard nearby, paying no attention to her yells. Mr Pails was shoved in, too, and the door was forced shut on them and locked.

George shouted at the top of her voice, and so did Mr Pails. But the shop was set apart from the others in the street, and there was no one to hear them on that hot, stifling afternoon.

George heard the sound of panting as the men removed the heavy little safe. Then the shop door shut, and there was the sound of the van being started up – and driven away!

'If only I'd had Timmy with me,' thought George fiercely, as she pushed hard against the door. 'Why did I say he could go and have an ice-cream with the others?'

Mr Pails was almost fainting with shock and fright, and was no help at all. George gave up struggling with the door after a while, and began to wish there weren't so many pans and brushes stored in the cupboard, leaving so little room for her and the old ironmonger!

She wondered what the others were doing. Would they come back and look for her? If they did, she could yell again.

But the others had now finished their ice-creams and were on the way to Windy Cove. George had said she didn't want an ice-cream, but would catch them up. Very well, they would walk on and she could overtake them.

So off they went along the road that led to Windy Cove, Timmy lagging behind a little on the lookout for his beloved George. Why didn't she come? He suddenly decided to go back and look for her. He felt anxious, although he didn't know why. He turned tail and trotted off back to the village.

'There goes Tim,' said Anne with a laugh. 'He can't bear to be without George for more than half an hour! Goodbye, Tim! Tell George to hurry up!'

They went on their way without Timmy, walking in a line across a narrow lane. Suddenly a van turned a corner behind them and came racing up at top speed. Dick only just dragged Anne out of its way in time. The van swerved and went on, hooting wildly at the next corner.

'What does the driver think he's doing?' said Dick angrily. 'Tearing down narrow, winding lanes like that! What's his hurry?'

The van turned the corner – and almost immediately after there came an explosive noise and the scream of brakes. Then a silence.

'Whew! That sounded like a burst tyre,' said Julian, beginning to run. 'I hope they haven't had an accident.'

The three turned the corner. They saw the van slewed round in the lane, almost in the ditch. The tyre on the left-hand back wheel was flat and had split badly. It certainly was a very burst tyre indeed! Two men were looking at it angrily.

'Here, you!' said one of the men, turning to Dick. 'Run to the nearest garage, will you, and ask a man to come and help us?'

'Definitely not!' said Dick. 'You nearly knocked over my sister just now. One of *you* can go and get help yourselves. You'd no right to drive along a country lane like that.'

But neither of the men made a move to go back for help. Instead, they scowled at the burst tyre and at each other. The three stood there, looking with interest at the angry men.

'You clear off,' said one of the men at last. 'Unless you want to help us with the wheel. Do you know how to change a wheel?'

'Yes,' said Julian, sitting down on the hedge bank. 'Don't *you*? It's funny if you don't know.

As your job is driving a van, I'd have thought it'd be one of the first things you'd learn!'

'You shut up,' said the first man, 'and clear off.'

'Why?' said Dick, sitting down beside Julian. 'You seem very keen to get rid of us, don't you? Or do you feel nervous that experts like us should watch you making a mess of such a simple thing as changing a wheel?'

Anne didn't like all this. 'I think I'll go back and meet George,' she said, and walked round the van. She took a quick look inside – and saw a little black safe there! A *safe*! She took a quick glance back at the two men. They certainly were a nasty-looking couple. She went over to Julian and sat down beside him. She took a twig and began to write idly in the thick dust at their feet, nudging him as she did so.

Julian looked down into the dust at once. 'A safe is in the van,' Anne had written in the dust, and, as soon as she knew that the boys had seen what she had written, she rubbed her foot over the hurried writing.

The three stared at the two men, who were now trying to change the wheel. It was obvious that they had never changed one before! Julian caught hold of Anne when she got up to go back and meet George.

'No. Stay,' he said. 'George may have changed her mind and gone home. You stay with us, Anne.'

So Anne stayed, hoping against hope that George would soon appear with Timmy. Why was she so long? She must have gone home, after all! What was Julian going to do? Wait for another car to come along, and then stop it and pass on his suspicions to the driver? Because the whole thing *was* very suspicious! Anne was certain that both safe and van were stolen. Where *was* George? She had had plenty of time to borrow scissors, cut her hair and catch them up!

Poor George had stood in the cupboard till she was so cramped that she could hardly move an arm or leg. Mr Pails seemed to have fainted, but she couldn't do anything about it. And then she heard a very familiar and welcome sound!

Feet pattered down the passage that led to the back of the shop, and then came a whine. Timmy!

'Timmy! Tim, I'm here, in this cupboard!' called George. 'Timmy!'

Timmy came and scraped at the cupboard, and then began to bark so furiously that a passer-by stopped in surprise. He pushed at the door, which had been left unlocked by the two thieves, and looked inside. He saw Timmy at once. The dog ran to him and then back to the cupboard, still barking.

'Anyone here?' called the passer-by.

'Yes, yes – we're locked in this cupboard!' cried George. 'Let us out, please.'

It took only two seconds for the man to run across the floor and unlock the cupboard. George staggered out, and Timmy flung himself on her, licking her from head to foot. Mr Pails was then dragged out, but he was so shocked and upset that it was difficult to get anything out of him.

'Police!' he kept saying. 'Police!'

'I'll send someone for the police – and a doctor, too,' said the man. 'You sit down in that chair, Mr Pails. I'll look after you.'

George slipped out of the shop. She felt rather faint after her long stay in the cramped cupboard.

She must hurry after the others, tell them what had happened, and get them to come back to the shop. It was no use going to Windy Cove that afternoon!

So she and Timmy hurried down the dusty lane that led from the village to Windy Cove. How far had the others got? Perhaps they were at the cove now!

But they weren't. They were still sitting at the side of the lane, watching two perspiring, harassed, fumbling men trying to put on a second wheel after having spent ages getting the first one off! There weren't enough tools to do the job properly, as Julian could very well see. He wished George would come. Timmy would be such a help!

And then, round the corner came George at last, with Timmy at her heels. Rather a pale George, evidently bursting with news. She raced up to them.

'Guess what happened to me? Mr Pails and I were locked in a cupboard in his shop by two thieves who . . .'

She suddenly caught sight of the two men tinkering with the van, and stopped, astounded. She pointed at them and shouted.

'Those are the two men! And that's the van they came in – have they got a safe in it?'

'Yes,' said Julian, standing up very suddenly. 'They have! Are you sure you recognize these men, George?'

'Oh *yes*! I'll never forget them all my life!' cried George. 'Timmy – watch them! Watch them, Timmy!'

Timmy sprang over to the two men, growling so fiercely and showing all his white teeth in such a snarl that the two men shrank back, terrified. One raised a hand as if to strike Timmy with the tool he held.

'If you hit him, he'll have you down on the ground at once,' warned George grimly, and the man dropped his hand. 'Now – what do we do, Julian? These men ought to be handed over to the police.'

'Listen – here comes a car,' said Dick. 'We can stop it and send a message back to the village.'

A big car came round the corner from the direction of Windy Cove. Julian waved to it to stop. Two men were in it.

'What's up?' they called.

Julian explained as shortly as he could. One of

the men jumped down immediately. 'You want the police at once,' he said. 'Let's put that wheel on, and take the two men back to Kirrin Village. My friend can drive the van, and the boy with the dog can go in the van with them! You others can get into my car, and we'll follow the van back to Kirrin and get the police!'

This all sounded very sane and sensible. The wheel was put on in a flash, the two men bundled into the back of the van with a snarling Timmy, and George (pleased because she had been mistaken for a boy!) sat in the front of the van with the man from the other car. They drove off, followed by the big car, in which were a pleased and smiling Julian, Dick and Anne!

It was very exciting when they all got to Kirrin Village! The police were amazed and delighted to have the two robbers safely delivered to them, with the safe *and* the stolen van as well! Mr Pails was very, very grateful. Timmy was half sorry he hadn't been allowed even a small bite, but extremely happy to have been able to rescue his beloved George!

'Well – what a thrill!' said George's mother, when they arrived home at last and told their astonishing tale. 'So you didn't get to Windy Cove, after all. Still – you can all go tomorrow!'

'I can't,' said George at once.

'WHY?' asked everyone, surprised.

'Because – I absolutely – *must* – get – my – hair – cut!' said George. 'And I'll make sure I'm not locked in a cupboard *next* time!'

3 Good old Timmy!

'Aren't you ready to come down to the beach and swim, Anne?' yelled George, standing at the bottom of the stairs. 'We're all waiting for you. HURRY UP!'

The study door flew open and Mr Kirrin, George's father, appeared. '*Georgina*! Will you *stop* shouting all day long? How can I work? For pity's sake, clear out of the house.'

'We're just going, Dad – and we're taking a picnic lunch so we won't be disturbing you for some time. I know you're on a big job – it's bad luck it's holiday time and we're here!'

He grunted and disappeared into his study. George's mother appeared with two big bags of sandwiches. 'Oh dear – was that your father shouting again?' she said. 'Never mind! He doesn't *mean* to be bad-tempered – but he really *is* on a big job at the moment, and he's trying to get some figures for the scientist he's working with, a Professor Humes, who's staying in Kirrin – at the Rollins Hotel. Now – here are your sandwiches – and biscuits and apples – and you can take some bottles of ginger beer out of the larder.'

Just then Anne raced down the stairs, and the Five, all in their swimming things, went off to the beach to swim and laze and play games on the sands. Only three people were there – two men and a lonely looking boy. Julian found a shaded cave and put the food on a shelf of rock.

'What about a swim straight away?' he said. 'Look – Timmy's off to rub noses with that dog we saw yesterday – the big ugly one we didn't much like. He belongs to those two men. They're not much to look at either! I wouldn't like to meet *them* on a dark night!'

'Well, Timmy seems to like their dog all right,' said George, staring at the two dogs sniffing at one another, then tearing along the sands together, barking happily.

'Look,' said Dick, 'there's that kid coming along the beach again, the one we saw yesterday. Shall we ask him to come swimming with us – he seems to be all on his own. Look out, kid – don't get knocked over by our dog!'

Timmy had come racing up joyfully, chasing the other dog, and the boy went sprawling as they galloped round him. Timmy turned in surprise and saw the boy rolling over and over on the sand. He gave an apologetic bark, and ran to the small boy, licking and sniffing at him.

The boy was terrified of Timmy. He began to scream in terror, and Julian ran to him. 'He's only making friends, he's only saying he's sorry he knocked you over, he won't hurt you! Come on, get up – we were just going to ask you to come and swim with us.'

'Oh,' said the boy, and stood up, shaking the sand off himself. He looked to be about nine or ten, and small for his age. 'Well – thanks. I'd like to swim with you. I'm Oliver Humes, and I'm staying at the Rollins Hotel.'

'Then your dad must be a friend of our uncle,' said Dick. 'He's called Kirrin – Quentin Kirrin – and he's a scientist. So is your dad, isn't he?'

'Yes. A very good one too,' said Oliver proudly. 'But he's worried this morning.'

'Why? What's up?' said George.

'Well – he's working on something important,'

said Oliver, 'and this morning he had a horrible letter. It said that unless Dad agreed to give the writer information he wanted about what Dad was working on, he'd – he'd kidnap me!'

'Oh rubbish!' said Julian. 'Don't you worry about that! We'll tell our dog Timmy to look after you. Just look at him playing with that ugly great mongrel. Timmy's a mongrel too – but we think he's beautiful!'

'I think he's too big,' said Oliver, fearfully, as Timmy came running up, panting. The other dog went back to the two men, who had just whistled for him.

'Come on – let's swim,' said Dick.

'I can't swim,' said Oliver. 'I wish you'd teach me.'

'Right. We will when we've had our swim,' said Anne. 'We'll go into the water now. Come on!'

And soon the Five, Timmy too, were splashing in the sea, yelling and diving in and out, having a glorious time, while Oliver paddled near the shore. Then suddenly Julian gave a shout, and pointed to the beach.

'Look! What's happening there? Hey!'

All the Five looked, and saw something very surprising! The two men who owned the big brown dog were dragging Oliver out of the water, one with his hand over the boy's mouth.

'They're kidnapping him! Remember that threatening letter he told us about, that his dad got this morning? Come on, quick – see if we can stop them. TIMMY! Come on, now!'

They swam to the shore and slipped hurriedly into their sandals.

'They've taken the kid up the cliffs – they're at the top, look!' panted Julian. 'After them, Timmy!'

But not even Timmy could get up the cliffs in time to rescue the screaming boy. Julian was at the top first, with Timmy – just in time to see a car driving off. The big dog was galloping after it.

'Why didn't they take the dog in the car, too?' wondered Dick.

'Perhaps he's a car-sick dog?' said Anne. 'Anyway, I bet he knows where the men are going, and has been ordered to follow. If the car doesn't go too fast he can easily keep up.'

'I've got the number, anyway,' said Dick.

'Listen – I think Anne's right when she says the dog must know where the men are going,' said Julian. 'And it *can't* be far away if the dog has to run the whole distance.'

Timmy wasn't listening. He was sniffing the ground here and there. Then he suddenly began to trot along the cliff-road, nose to ground.

George gave a sudden exclamation. 'I know! He's sniffing the other dog's tracks – he knows his smell, and he's following it!'

'You're right! Look – let's see if he'll follow the trail properly,' said Julian. 'He might lead us to Oliver! Tell him, George. He always understands every word you say.'

'Timmy! Listen!' said George, and pointed to some paw marks made in the sandy road by the big mongrel dog. 'Follow, Timmy, follow. Understand?'

Timmy lifted his big head and looked hard at George, his ears pricked up, his head on one side. Yes – he understood. Then, with nose to ground he trotted swiftly away down the cliff-road, sniffing the tracks of the other dog. How did he do it? What a nose Timmy had!

'Come on,' said Dick. 'Timmy will lead us to

wherever those men are taking Oliver.'

Very steadily, Timmy followed the scent down the cliff-road, turned off to the left, trotted down a lane, swung to the right, then to the left. He waited at the traffic lights, and when they changed to green, he crossed the road, and then trotted right through the town, nose to trail! The children padded behind in their swimming things, Anne getting very puffed!

At the other end of the town Timmy turned to the left and padded down a lane, nose still on the scent! The four followed closely.

'I'll have to have a rest soon,' panted Anne.

'Hey, that's the car that took the boy away!' exclaimed Dick, suddenly, as they passed a garage, outside which stood a black car, taking in petrol. 'The men are in it. But I can't see Oliver – and that great dog isn't anywhere about, either.'

'Well, they must have hidden Oliver somewhere not far off, and then they came back here for petrol,' said Julian. 'Go on, Tim – you're on the right trail. I expect they've left that dog in charge of the boy. I bet if anyone went near, he'd tear them to pieces!'

'And *I* don't want Timmy in a dogfight,' said George.

'Yes. Not so good,' said Julian, and came to a stop. Timmy, however, went on, and wouldn't come back, even though George called him.

'Obstinate thing!' said George crossly. 'Once he's following a trail nothing on earth will stop him. Well – I'm going after him in case he gets into trouble!'

'Look – Timmy's gone through that gateway,' said Anne, 'into a field. There's a shed at the bottom of it. Could Oliver be there, with the dog inside, guarding him?'

Timmy stopped suddenly and began to growl. George ran to catch hold of his collar. But Timmy wrenched himself away and raced to the shed, scraping at the wooden door. Immediately a volley of fierce barks came from the shed. The Five halted.

A voice came from the shed. 'Help! Help, I'm locked in here!'

'There – Timmy followed the trail correctly!' said George. 'Quick, Ju – we mustn't let him break in that door – the other dog will fly at him, and at us, too! Whatever can we do?'

It was obvious that the other dog had been left on guard, and would fling himself on anyone or anything that tried to prevent him from doing his duty.

'TIMMY! STOP THROWING YOURSELF AGAINST THAT DOOR!' yelled George. 'YOU'LL BREAK IT DOWN, AND THEN GOODNESS KNOWS WHAT'LL HAPPEN!'

As both dogs, barking fiercely, again flung themselves on it from opposite sides, the door cracked in two places – and the bottom half shook and shivered! 'Anne, George, quick, come with me!' said Julian. 'We may be attacked by that dog once he gets out! Run! We could perhaps climb that tree, look. Hurry up, for goodness' sake!'

Terrified, they all raced for the tree, and clambered up on the branches.

CRASH! The door fell to the ground, broken in half. At once the great mongrel leapt out. But it took absolutely no notice of Timmy. It ran instead to the tree and stood below, growling fiercely. Timmy stood staring in surprise. Why was this dog growling at the children? It was all a mistake, Timmy decided, and he must put it right.

He ran to the tree, and whined as if to say: 'It's all right. Please come down and play with us!' Then he went to the other dog, and whined to him too.

The mongrel gave a loud bark, and jumped up. He ran off a little, stopped and turned round as if saying to Timmy: 'All right – you want a game? Then so do I! You're the dog I played with this morning, aren't you? Well, come on, let's have a game!'

And, to the children's enormous astonishment the two dogs gambolled amiably together!

'I feel a bit silly up here,' said Dick, climbing down. 'Come on – the war's over. Those dogs look as if they're friends for life. Let's go and get that kid.'

With the frightened boy safely in their midst, they began to walk cautiously out of the field. The two dogs took absolutely no notice! The big mongrel had got Timmy down on the ground, and was pretending to worry him. Timmy was having the time of his life!

'Look – there's a bus going to Kirrin!' said Julian, delighted. 'Stop it! We'll get in and take

Oliver back to safety while we've a chance. Timmy will just have to walk. He'll make that dog forget all about guarding Oliver!'

It wasn't very long before they were safely back in Kirrin. Oliver looked very white, but when Julian told him solemnly that it was really a Very Big Adventure, he cheered up and began to boast! 'I was *kidnapped*! What will the boys at school say? But I was really scared though. Can we go and find my dad?'

Professor Humes was very thankful to see his son again, for already he had notified the police that he had disappeared. Dick gave the police the number of the men's car.

'You'll soon track that all right!' he said. 'But not as well as Tim here – he used his nose, and a very good nose it is too!'

'Woof!' said Timmy, and let his tongue hang out of his mouth.

'He says he's hot and thirsty,' said George. 'Let's buy him an ice-cream.'

'We'll ALL have the biggest ice-creams there are in the village shop,' said the Professor, patting Timmy. 'I could do with one myself.'

'I could do with four,' said Oliver, 'so I hope

you're feeling generous, Dad! Dad, Timmy's a wonder dog!'

'Well, we've always known *that*,' said George. 'Come on, Timmy – ICE-CREAMS!'

4 A lazy afternoon

'It's hot!' said Julian, fanning himself with a paper. 'What are we all going to do this afternoon?'

'Nothing!' said Dick at once. 'I feel as if I'm rapidly melting. It's even too hot to go swimming.'

'Let's have a *lazy* afternoon for once,' said George. 'If anyone suggests a walk or a bike ride in this heat, I'll scream.'

'Woof,' said Timmy at once.

'He's suggesting a *walk*, George,' said Anne, with a laugh. 'Scream!'

'Too hot even for that,' said George. 'Let's find a cool, shady place, take our books, and either read or snooze till tea-time. I'd enjoy a lazy afternoon for once.'

'Woof,' said Timmy mournfully, not agreeing at all.

'Come on, then,' said Julian. 'We'll go to that little copse we know, under those leafy trees –

near that tiny stream that ripples along and makes a nice cool noise!'

'Well – I think I can just about walk there,' said Dick, and they all set off, strolling along, unable to keep up with the lively, energetic Timmy.

'It makes me hot even to look at Timmy,' complained Dick. 'Hot to hear him too, puffing like a steam-train. Put your tongue in, Timmy, I can't bear to look at it.'

Timmy ran ahead, glad that they were off for what appeared to be a walk. He was very disappointed when the others flopped down in a little copse under some big leafy trees near a small brook. He stood looking at them in disgust.

'Sorry, Tim. No walkies, ' said George. 'Come and sit down with us. For goodness' sake, don't go rabbiting in this weather.'

'It'd be a waste of your time, Timmy,' said Dick. 'All sensible bunnies are having an afternoon snooze, down at the bottom of their holes, waiting for the cool evening to come.'

'Woof,' said Timmy in scorn, watching the four arrange themselves comfortably under a canopy made by young saplings and bushes. Branches from big trees nearby overhung them, and by the time the four had wriggled themselves well into the little thicket, not a single sunbeam could reach them. In fact, it was difficult to see them, so well hidden were they in the green shade.

'This is better,' said George. 'I think it's about the coolest spot we'll find anywhere. Doesn't that little stream sound nice, too, gurgling away over the stones. I think I'm going to sleep – and if you dare to flop yourself down on my middle, Timmy, I'll send you home!'

Timmy stood and looked at the well-hidden four. His tail drooped. What was the point of coming to a wood, to lie down and do nothing? Well – *he* was going rabbiting! He swung round, pushed his way out of the thicket, and disappeared. George raised her head to look after him.

'He's gone rabbiting after all,' she said. 'Well, I hope he remembers where we are and comes back at tea-time. Now for a lazy – peaceful – quiet afternoon!'

'Don't talk so much,' said Dick, and got a sideways kick from George's foot. 'Oh, I feel sleepy!'

In a few minutes' time not one of the four was awake. Books lay unopened on the ground. A small beetle ran over Anne's bare leg, and she didn't even feel it. A robin hopped on to a branch just above Dick's face, but his eyes were closed and he didn't see it.

It certainly was a hot afternoon. Nobody was about at all. Not a sound was to be heard except for the running water nearby, and a yellowhammer somewhere who persisted in saying that he wanted 'a little bit of bread and no cheese'. The four were as sound asleep as if they were in bed.

And then, far away on a road that bordered the wood, a motorbike came by. It had a sidecar, and it made quite a noise. But the four sleepers heard nothing. They didn't know that the motorbike had slowed down and turned into the wood, taking one of the grassy woodland walks that wound here and there, quiet and cool.

The motorbike came slowly down one of the paths, not making very much noise now, because it was going slowly. It came near to the little copse where the children lay hidden in the cool shade of the bushes.

The engine of the motorbike gave a sudden little cough as it came along, and Julian awoke with a start. What was that noise? He listened, but he could hear nothing more because the motorbike, with its sidecar, had now stopped. Julian shut his eyes again.

But he opened them immediately because he heard voices – low voices. People must be somewhere near. Where were they? Julian hoped they wouldn't disturb the four in their cool hiding place. He made a little peephole in the bush he was lying under, and spied through it.

He saw the motorbike and sidecar on the grassy path some way off. He saw two men, one just getting out of the sidecar. Julian didn't like the look of them at all.

'What nasty-looking men!' he thought. 'What are they doing here in the middle of a summer's afternoon?'

At first the men talked in low voices, and then an argument started. One raised his voice. 'I tell you, we were followed! It's the only thing to do, to come here and dump the stuff!'

A small bag was dragged out of the sidecar. The second man seemed to be grumbling, not at all willing to do what the other wanted.

'I tell you, I *know* it won't be found if we put it there,' said the first man. 'What's the matter with you? We can't afford to be stopped with the stuff on us – and I *know* we were being followed. It was only because we crossed against those traffic lights that we got away.'

Julian awoke the others, and whispered to them. Something strange was happening! Soon all the four were peeping through leafy peepholes at what was going on. They saw what looked like a small mailbag on the ground by the motorbike.

'What are they going to do with it?' whispered George. 'Should we burst out on them?'

'I would if we had Timmy with us,' whispered back Julian. 'But he's gone rabbiting and may be miles away.'

'And these crooks would be more than a match for us,' said Dick. 'We daren't even show ourselves. We can only watch.'

'I hope we see where they hide the stuff, whatever it is,' said Anne, trying to spy through the leaves. 'There they go with the bag.'

'I can see them,' said Dick, almost forgetting to whisper in his excitement. 'They're climbing a tree!'

'Yes – one's already up, and the other's

passing the bag to him,' whispered Julian. 'It must have a hollow trunk, I think. Oh, I wish Timmy was here!'

'Now the second man's trying to climb up, too,' said George. 'The first one wants help, I suppose. The bag must be stuck.'

Both men were now up the tree, trying to stuff the bag down some kind of hollow there. At last there was a thud as if the bag had dropped down.

'If *only* Timmy was here!' said Julian again. 'It's maddening to lie here and do nothing – but we'd be no match for those two men!'

Then a sudden noise came to their ears – the scampering of feet. Then came a familiar sound. 'Woof!'

'Timmy!' yelled Julian and George together, and Julian leapt up and pushed his way out of his hiding place at once. 'Tell Tim to guard that tree, George, quick!'

'Here, Timmy – on guard!' shouted George, and the astonished Timmy ran to the tree where the two men were staring down in sudden horror.

Timmy gave a blood-curdling growl, and

one man, who had been about to jump down, shrank back.

'Call that dog off!' he yelled. 'What do you think you're doing?'

'You tell us what *you're* doing,' said Julian. 'What's in the bag you pushed down that tree hollow?'

'What bag? What are you talking about? You must be mad!' said the man. 'Call that dog off, or I'll report you to the police.'

'Right! We'll report *you* at the same time!' said Julian. 'You'll stay up that tree till we bring the police back here – and I warn you, if you try jumping down and running away, you'll be sorry. You've no idea what sharp teeth that dog has!'

The two men were so angry that they could hardly speak. Timmy barked loudly, and kept leaping up to try to reach them. Julian turned to the others. 'Go to the main road and stop a car. Go to the nearest police station and tell the police there to send men here at once. Hurry up.'

But before the others could go off, there came the sound of another motorbike – and then a second – bumping along the woodland path. Julian fell silent. Were more crooks coming?

Timmy would be a great help, if so. Julian and the others got behind trees and watched to see who was on the coming motorbikes.

'The police!' yelled Dick, suddenly seeing the familiar uniform. 'They must have been the ones chasing those men. Somebody must have given them the tip that they had turned off into the wood! Hey! We can help you!'

The two policemen stopped in surprise. They saw the motorbike and sidecar. 'Have you kids seen anything of two men with a bag?' shouted one of them.

'Yes. The bag's stuffed down a tree over there, and our dog's guarding the men – they're up in the tree!' shouted back Julian, going towards the police. 'You've just come in time to collect them!'

'Good stuff!' said the policeman with a grin, as he saw the two scared men up the tree, with Timmy still leaping up hopefully at them. 'The bag's up there, too, is it?'

'Down in the hollow of the tree,' said Julian.

'Well, thanks very much for doing our job for us,' said the second policeman. 'We've got some pals on the main road, ' he said. 'We said we'd shout if we found anything. They'll soon be along.' He looked at the two men in the tree. 'Well, Jim and Stan? You thought you'd fooled us, didn't you? Are you coming quietly – or do we ask the dog to help us round you up?'

Jim and Stan took one look at the eager Timmy.

'We'll come quietly,' they said, and, when three more men came racing down the woodland path, there was no trouble at all. Jim and Stan went off with the policemen, Timmy gave one last fierce bark, and all Five watched the men, the motorbikes, and the sidecar disappear with many bumps up the path back to the main road.

'Well!' said George. 'Talk about a nice cool, lazy afternoon! I'm hotter than ever now!'

'Woof,' said Timmy, his tongue hanging out almost to the ground. He looked very hot, too.

'Well, you shouldn't go rabbiting,' said George. 'No wonder you're hot!'

'It's a very good thing he *did* go rabbiting!' said Dick. 'If he'd been with us, he'd have barked, and those men would have known we were here – and would have gone further on to hide their goods. We'd never have seen what they were doing, or have been able to catch them.'

'Yes. That's true,' said George, and patted Timmy. 'All right, Timmy – you were right to go rabbiting and to come back when you did!'

'Tea-time, everybody!' said Dick, looking at his watch. 'Well – what a very nice, peaceful, lazy afternoon! I really *have* enjoyed it!'

5 Well done, Famous Five!

'Nice to be together again,' said Julian. 'All Five of us!'

George nodded. 'Yes, Timmy's thrilled too. Aren't you, Tim?'

Timmy the dog barked, and laid his big head on George's knee, and she patted him. All the Five were on the top of Kirrin Hill, looking at the wide spread of country stretched out below them.

Anne was handing out the picnic food, and Dick passed it round. Timmy raised his head at once, and sniffed. Would there be anything for him?

'Of course, Timmy,' said Anne. 'A bone – and two big dog biscuits.'

'As well as a good part of our own sandwiches and buns, I expect,' said Dick. 'No, Tim – that pile's mine – and I'm *not* going to exchange my biscuits for yours!'

'What a wonderful view we've got from here,'

said Julian, beginning to munch his sandwich. 'We can see for miles and miles all round us.'

'Well – not much is happening,' said Anne, 'except that those sheep are ambling around that field, and those cows are doing what they always do – eat, eat, eat all day long – although if *I* had to eat nothing but grass, I'd soon stop!'

'Can't see a soul about,' said Dick, lazily. 'I suppose it's everyone's dinner-time. Now, why can't something exciting happen, just to give us a bit of interest while we're eating! We've had so many adventures that I'm beginning to feel quite cheated if one doesn't turn up as soon as we're together again!'

'Oh, for goodness' sake, don't wish for an adventure today!' said Anne. 'I like a bit of peace. I don't want to choke with excitement when I'm eating these delicious sandwiches! What *has* Aunt Fan put into them?'

'A bit of everything in the larder, I should think,' said George. 'Get away, Tim – don't breathe all over me like that!'

'What's that moving right away over there – along the side of that hill?' asked Dick, suddenly. 'Is it cows?'

Everyone looked. 'Too far away to see,' said George. 'Can't be cows, though – they don't move like cows – cows walk so slowly.'

'Well, they must be horses then,' said Julian.

'But who'd have so many horses out for exercise round here?' said George. 'All the horses are farm horses – they'd be working in the fields, not trotting in a row across a hillside.'

'It must be a riding school, idiot,' said Dick. 'If we had our binoculars, we'd see a lot of nicely behaved little girls from some nearby school cantering along on their nicely behaved horses!'

'I *did* bring my binoculars – didn't you notice?' said George, rummaging about behind her. 'I put them down here somewhere – ah, here they are. Want them, Dick?'

Dick took them and put them to his eyes. 'Yes – it's a line of horses – about six – wonderful ones too. But it's not girls who are riding them – it's boys – stable boys, I think.'

'Oh, of course – I forgot,' said George. 'They're wonderful racing horses from Lord Daniron's stable – they have to be exercised each day. Can you see a very big horse in the line, Dick? A magnificent creature – he's called Thunder-Along, and he's the most valuable horse in the country – so they say!'

Dick was now examining the horses with much interest, holding the binoculars to his eyes. 'They're *lovely* horses – and yes, I think I can see the one you mean, George. A great horse with a wonderful head – he's the first one of all.'

'Let me see,' said George, but Dick held on to the binoculars.

'No. Half a mo. Hey – something's happening! What is it? Something seemed to rush straight across in front of Thunder-Along – was it a fox or a dog? Oh, he's rearing up in fright, he's in quite a panic. He . . . He's off!' suddenly shouted Dick. 'He's thrown his groom – yes, he's on the ground, hurt, I think – and he's bolting! Oh no – he'll kill himself.'

A silence fell on the Five. Even Timmy was quiet, staring in the same direction as the others. George made as if to snatch her binoculars away from Dick, but he dodged, gluing them to his eyes.

'Don't lose sight of the horse, Dick, keep the binoculars on him,' said Julian, urgently. 'He's the finest horse this country has. Watch him –

watch where he goes! We may be the only people who can see the way he takes.'

'All right, all right,' said Dick, impatiently. 'Don't jog my arm, Anne. Yes – there he goes – he's scared! He's still bolting at top speed – I hope he doesn't run into a tree – no, he just missed that one. Oh, now he's come to a gate – a high gate . . .'

The others had now lost sight of the horse and were hanging on to every word of Dick's. Timmy was so excited that he began to bark, sensing the general excitement. George shushed him, fearing to lose something that Dick said.

'He's over the gate – what a jump, oh what a jump! Now he's galloping down the road – I can't see him – yes, there he is again – he's come to the stream – he's over it, cleared it beautifully – away he goes, up Rilling Hill – now he's going more slowly – he must be absolutely puffed. He's gone into a field of corn – the farmer won't like that! And now – he must be lying down in the corn! I can't see him any more!'

George snatched the binoculars from him – no, she couldn't see him either. She switched them to the hillside where the horses had been exercising.

What a commotion! The grooms were talking excitedly, pointing here and there, evidently at a loss to know where Thunder-Along had gone!

'I'm afraid this is the end of our picnic,' said Julian. 'As long as Thunder-Along is in the field of corn, resting, he's safe – but if he goes off again, anything may happen! We've got to report our news at once – and Dick, you'd better bike as fast as you can to that cornfield. Maybe the horse will still be there.'

Dick ran to where he had left his bike, and leapt on it. The others went to theirs, too, and soon they were riding off to Kirrin to report their news to the police, who would at once get in touch with the stables.

Dick planned out his way as he went. What would be the best way to get quickly to Rilling Hill? He soon made up his mind, and cycled along at top speed. It seemed a very long way – but at last he was cycling up the hill to where he hoped to find the field of corn. He was so out of breath that he had to get off his bike and walk. He came to the field-gate and looked in cautiously at the corn. He could see no horse at all – and no wonder, for he would be lying down!

'I'll have to tread in carefully,' thought Dick. 'I can see the way he trod – where the corn's flattened.' So in he went – only to hear a furious voice yelling at him from the gate behind him.

'Come out of that corn! Come out at once!' It was the farmer, red with anger. Dick didn't like to yell back, in case he frightened the horse. So he pointed urgently into the field and went carefully on.

'You wait!' yelled the farmer. 'I'll get the police on to you!'

Suddenly Dick saw the horse. It lay in the corn, ears pricked up, eyes rolling. Dick stopped.

'Well, old beauty?' he said. 'Well, you magnificent thing! Thunder-Along! Do you know your name? Poor boy, how frightened you were! Come now, come! You're safe – come along with me!'

To his surprise and delight the great horse stood up and flicked his ears to and fro, watching Dick carefully. Then he whinnied a little, and stepped towards him.

The boy took hold of the reins gently, and dared to rub the velvety nose. Then he led the horse carefully out of the corn. The farmer stood staring in amazement at the magnificent creature.

'But – but, isn't that Lord Daniron's horse, Thunder-Along?' he said, almost in a whisper. 'Did he bolt?'

Dick nodded his head. 'Keep my bike for me, will you?' he said. 'I must take the horse while he's quiet. I expect as soon as the owners know where he is, they'll send a horsebox. I'll lead him up and down the lane for a little, till they come.'

It wasn't long before a great horsebox drove slowly up the lane, and Thunder-Along's own groom came to pet him and lead him quietly into it. He ran his eyes over the horse carefully.

'No damage done!' he said. 'Thank goodness you had binoculars with you, boy, and saw where he went. You did well to get him!'

As soon as the horsebox had gone down the hill, Dick jumped on his bike and rode away. He soon met the others, cycling towards him, anxious to know what had happened. Timmy was running beside them.

'The horse was all right. I got him, and there's not a scratch on him!' said Dick. 'What a bit of luck we had this morning, looking through your binoculars, George! What do you say, Timmy?'

'Woof!' said Timmy, agreeing as usual, 'Woof!'

'He says it's the kind of thing that *would* happen to the Famous Five!' said George. And, of course, she was quite right!

6 *Five and a half-term adventure*

The Five were at Kirrin Cottage for a short half-term holiday. For once, both the boys' school and the girls' school had chosen the same weekend!

'It hardly ever happens that we can spend half-term together,' said Anne, stroking Timmy. 'And what luck to have such lovely weather at the beginning of November!'

'Four days off!' said George. 'What shall we do?'

'Swim!' said Julian and Dick together.

'*What*!' said their aunt, horrified, 'Swim in November! You must be mad! I can't allow that, Julian, really I can't.'

'All right,' said Julian, grinning at his aunt. 'Don't worry. We haven't got our swimming things here.'

'Let's walk over to Windy Hill,' said Dick. 'It's a wonderful walk, by the sea most of the way. And there may be blackberries and nuts still to find. I'd like a good walk.'

'Woof,' said Timmy at once, and put his big paw up on Dick's knee. He was always hoping to hear that magic word 'Walk'!

'Yes, let's do that,' said Anne. 'Aunt Fanny, shall we take a picnic lunch – or is it too much bother to prepare?'

'Not if you help me,' said her aunt, getting up. 'Come along – we'll see what we can find. But remember that it gets dark very quickly in the afternoon now, so don't leave it too late when you turn back.'

The Five set off half an hour later, with sandwiches and slices of fruitcake in a rucksack carried by Julian. Dick had a basket for any nuts or blackberries. His aunt had promised a blackberry-and-apple pie if they *did* find any berries for picking.

Timmy was very happy. He trotted along with the others, sniffing here and there, and barking at a curled-up hedgehog in a hole in a bank.

'Now, leave it alone,' said George. 'You really should have learnt by now that hedgehogs aren't meant to be carried in your mouth, Timmy! Don't wake it up – it's gone to sleep for the winter!'

'It's a gorgeous day for the beginning of November,' said Anne. 'The trees still have their leaves – all colours: red, yellow, brown, pink – and the beeches are the colour of gold.'

'Blackberries!' said Dick, catching sight of a bush whose sprays were still covered with the black fruit. 'Taste them – they're as sweet as sugar!'

As soon as the blackberries were to be seen on bushes here and there, the Five slowed up considerably! The blackberries that were still left were big and full of sweetness.

'They melt in my mouth!' said George. 'Try one, Timmy!' But Timmy spat the blackberry out in disgust.

'Manners, Timmy, manners!' said Dick at once, and Timmy wagged his big tail and pranced round joyfully.

It was a good walk but a slow one. They found a hazelnut copse and filled the basket with nuts that had fallen to the ground. Two red squirrels sat up in a nearby tree and chattered at them crossly. This was *their* nut copse!

'You can spare us a few!' called Anne. 'I expect you've got hundreds hidden away safely for the winter.'

They had their lunch on the top of Windy Hill. It wasn't a windy day, but, all the same, there was a good breeze on the top, and Julian decided to sit behind a big gorse bush for shelter.

'We'll be in the sun and out of the wind then,' he said. 'Spread out the lunch, Anne!'

'I feel *really* hungry!' said George. 'I can't believe it's only just one o'clock, Julian.'

'Well, that's what my watch says,' said Julian, taking a sandwich. 'Ha – ham and lettuce together – just what I like. Get away, Tim – I can't eat with you trying to nibble my sandwich too.'

It was a magnificent view from the top of the hill. The four children munched their sandwiches and gazed down into the valley below. A town lay there, comfortably sprawled in the shelter of the hills. Smoke rose lazily from the chimneys.

'Look – there's a train running along the railway line down there,' said George, waving her sandwich in its direction. 'It looks just like a toy one.'

'It's going to Beckton,' said Julian. 'See – there's the station – it's stopping there. It really *does* look like a toy train!'

'Now it's off again – on its way to Kirrin, I

suppose,' said Dick. 'Any more sandwiches? What, none? Shame! I'll have a slice of cake, then – hand it over, Anne.'

They talked lazily, enjoying being together again. Timmy wandered from one to the other, getting a titbit here and a scrap of ham there.

'I *think* I can see another nut copse over yonder – the other side of the hill,' said George. 'I vote we go and see what nuts we can find – and then I suppose we ought to be thinking of going back home. The sun's getting very low, Ju.'

'Yes, it is, considering it's only about two o'clock,' said Julian, looking at the red November sun hardly showing above the horizon. 'Come on, then – let's get a few more nuts, and then go back home. I love that long path winding over the cliffs beside the sea.'

They all went off to the little copse, and to their delight, found a wonderful crop of hazelnuts there. Timmy nosed about in the grass and brought mouthfuls of the nuts to George.

'Thanks, Timmy,' said George. 'Very clever of you – but I wish you could tell the bad ones from the good ones!'

'Hey,' said Dick, after a while, 'the sun's gone,

and it's getting dark. Julian, are you sure your watch is right?'

Julian looked at his watch. 'It says just about two o'clock still,' he said in surprise. 'Oh – I must have forgotten to wind it up or something. It's definitely stopped now – and it must have been very slow before!'

'Idiot,' said Dick. 'No wonder George thought it was long past lunch-time when you said it was one o'clock. We'll never get home before dark now – and we haven't any torches with us.'

'That cliff-path isn't too good to walk along in the dark, either,' said Anne. 'It goes so near the edge at times.'

'We'd better start back immediately,' said Julian. 'I'm really sorry about this – I never dreamt that my watch was wrong.'

'I tell you what would be a better idea,' said George. 'Why don't we just take the path down into Beckton and catch the train to Kirrin? We'll be so late if we walk back, and Mum'll be ringing up the police about us!'

'Good idea of yours, George,' said Julian. 'Come on – let's take the path while we can still see. It leads straight down to the town.'

So away went the Five as fast as they could. It was dark when they reached the town, but that didn't matter, because the street lamps were on. They made their way to the station, half running down the main street.

'Look – Robin Hood's on at the cinema here,' said Anne. 'Look at the posters!'

'And what's that on at the hall over there?' said George. 'Timmy, come here – oh, he's shot across the road. Come HERE, Timmy!'

But Timmy was running up the steps of the Town Hall. Julian gave a sudden laugh. 'Look – there's a big dog show on there – and Timmy must have thought he ought to go in for it!'

'He smelt the dogs there,' said George, rather cross. 'Come on – let's get him, or we'll lose the next train.'

The hall was plastered with posters of dogs of all kinds. Julian stopped to read them while George went in after Timmy.

'Some very valuable dogs here,' he said. 'Some beauties, too – look at the picture of this white poodle. Ah – here comes Tim again, looking very sorry for himself. I bet he knows he wouldn't win a single prize – except for brains!'

'It was the doggy smell that made him go to see what was on,' said George. 'He was really cross because they wouldn't let him in.'

'Hurry up – I think I can hear a train coming!' said Dick, and they all raced down the road to the station, which was quite near. The train puffed in as they went to buy their tickets. The guard was blowing his whistle and waving his flag as they rushed on to the platform. Dick pulled open the door of the very last compartment and they all bundled in, panting.

'That was close,' said Dick, half falling on to a seat. 'Look out, Tim – you nearly had me over.'

The four children got back their breath and looked round the carriage. It wasn't empty, as they had expected. Two other people were there, sitting at the opposite end, facing each other – a man and a woman. They looked at the Five, annoyed.

'Oh,' said Anne, seeing the woman carrying a shawled bundle in her arms, 'I hope we haven't woken your baby. We only *just* caught the train.'

The woman rocked the little thing in her arms, and crooned to it, covering its head with a shawl – a rather dirty one, Anne noticed.

'Is she all right?' asked the man. 'Cover her up more – it's cold in here.'

'There, there now,' crooned the woman, pulling the shawl tighter. The children lost interest and began to talk. Timmy sat still by George, very bored. Then he suddenly sniffed round, and went over to the woman. He leapt up on to the seat beside her and pawed at the shawl! The woman shrieked and the man shouted at Timmy.

'Stop that! Get down! Here, you kids, look after that great dog of yours. It'll frighten the baby into fits!'

'Come here, Timmy,' said George at once, surprised that he was interested in a baby.

Timmy whined and went to George, looking back at the woman. A tiny whimpering noise came from the shawl, and the woman frowned.

'You've waked her,' she said, and began to talk to the man in a loud, harsh voice.

Timmy was very disobedient! Before George could stop him, he was up on the seat again, pawing at the woman and whining. The man leapt up furiously.

'Don't hit my dog, don't hit him, he'll snap at you!' shouted George – and mercifully, just at that moment the train drew in at a station.

'Let's get out and go into another carriage,' said Anne, and opened the door. The four of them, followed by a very unwilling Timmy, were soon getting into a compartment near the engine. George looked crossly at Timmy.

'Whatever came over you, Tim?' she said. 'You're never interested in babies! Now sit down and don't move!'

Timmy was surprised at George's cross voice, and he crept under the seat and stayed there. The train came to a little station, where there was a small platform, and stopped to let a few people get out.

'It's Seagreen Halt,' said Dick, looking out. 'And there go the man and woman and baby – I wouldn't like them for a mum and dad!'

'It's quite dark now,' said George, looking through the window. 'It's a good thing we just caught the train. Mum'll be getting worried.'

It was nice to be in the cosy sitting room at Kirrin Cottage again, eating an enormous tea and telling George's mother about their walk. She was very pleased with the nuts and blackberries. They told her about the man and woman and baby, too, and how funny Timmy had been, pawing at the shawl.

'He was funny before that,' said Anne, remembering. 'Aunt Fanny, there was a dog show on at Beckton, and Timmy must have read the posters, and thought he could go in for it – because he suddenly dashed across the road and into the Town Hall where the show was being held!'

'Really?' said her aunt, laughing. 'Well, perhaps he went to see if he could find the beautiful little white Pekinese that was stolen there today! Mrs Harris rang up and told me about it – there was such a to-do. The little dog, which was worth five thousand pounds, was cuddled down in its basket one minute – and the next it was gone! Nobody was seen to take it, and although they hunted in every corner of the hall, there was no sign of the dog.'

'What a mystery!' said Anne. 'How could anyone possibly take a dog like that away without being seen?'

'Easy,' said Dick. 'Wrap it in a coat, or pop it into a shopping basket and cover it up. Then walk through the crowd and out of the hall!'

'Or wrap it in a shawl and pretend it was a

baby – like the little one in that dirty shawl in the train,' said Anne. 'I mean – we *thought* that was a baby, of course – but it could easily have been a dog – or a cat – or even a monkey. We couldn't see its face!'

There was a sudden silence. Everyone was staring at Anne and thinking hard. Julian banged his hand on the table and made everyone jump.

'There's something in what Anne has just said,' he said. 'Something worth thinking about! Did anyone see even a *glimpse* of the baby's face – or hair? Did you, Anne – you were nearest?'

'No,' said Anne, quite startled. 'No, I didn't. I did try to see, because I like babies – but the shawl was pulled right over the face and head.'

'And don't you remember how interested *Timmy* was in it?' said George, excited. 'He's never interested in babies – but he kept *on* jumping up and pawing at the shawl.'

'And do you remember how the baby whimpered?' said Dick. 'It was much more like a little dog whining than a baby, now I come to think of it. No wonder Timmy was excited! He *knew* it was a dog by the smell!'

'Wow! This is really exciting,' said Julian,

getting up. 'I vote we go to Seagreen Halt and snoop round the tiny village there.'

'*No,*' said Aunt Fanny firmly. 'I won't have that, Julian. It's pitch-dark outside, and I don't want you snooping round for dog thieves on your half-term holiday.'

'Oh!' said Julian, bitterly disappointed.

'Ring up the police,' said his aunt. 'Tell them what you've just told me – they'll be able to find out the truth very quickly. They'll be sure to know who has a baby and who hasn't – they can go round snooping quite safely!'

'All right,' said Julian, sad to have a promising adventure snatched away so quickly. He went to the phone, frowning. Aunt Fanny *could* have let him and Dick slip out to Seagreen in the dark – it would have been such fun.

The police were very interested and asked a lot of questions. Julian told them all he knew, and everyone listened intently. Then Julian put down the receiver and turned to the others, looking quite cheerful again.

'They were very interested,' he said. 'And they're off to Seagreen Village straightaway in the police car. They're going to let us know what they find. Aunt Fanny – we CANNOT go to bed tonight till we know what happens!'

'No, we can't!' cried all the others, and Timmy joined in with a bark, leaping round excitedly.

'Very well,' said Aunt Fanny, smiling. 'What a collection of children you are – you can't even go for a walk without something happening! Now – get out the cards and let's have a game.'

They played cards, with their ears listening for the phone. But it didn't ring. Supper-time came and still it hadn't rung.

'It's no good,' said Dick gloomily. 'We probably made a mistake.'

Timmy suddenly began to bark, and then ran to the door, pawing at it.

'Someone's coming,' said George. 'Listen – it's a car!'

They all listened, and heard the car stop at the gate – then footsteps came up the path and the doorbell rang. George was out in a flash, and opened it.

'Oh – it's the police!' she called. 'Come in, do come in.'

A burly policeman came in, followed by another. The second one carried a bundle in a shawl! Timmy leapt up to it at once, whining!

'Oh! It *wasn't* a baby, then!' cried Anne, and the policeman smiled and shook his head. He pulled the shawl away – and there, fast asleep, was a tiny white Pekinese, its little snub nose tucked into the shawl!

'Oh – the darling!' said Anne. 'Wake up, you funny little thing!'

'It's been doped,' said the policeman. 'I suppose they were afraid of it whining in the night and giving its hiding place away!'

'Tell us what happened,' begged Dick. 'Get down, Timmy. George, he's getting too excited – he wants the Peke to play with him!'

'Acting on your information we went to Seagreen,' said the policeman. 'We asked the porter what people got out of the train this evening, and if anyone carried a baby – and he said four people got out – and two of them were a man and woman, and the woman carried a baby in a shawl. He told us who they were – so away we went to the cottage . . .'

'Woof,' said Timmy interrupting, trying to get at the tiny dog again, but nobody took any notice of him.

'We looked through the back window of the cottage,' went on the policeman, 'and spotted what we wanted at once! The woman was giving the dog a drink of milk in a saucer – and she must have put some drug into it, because the little thing dropped down and fell asleep at once while we were watching.'

'So in we went, and that was that,' said the second policeman, smiling round. 'The couple were so scared that they blurted out everything – how someone had paid them to steal the dog, and how they had taken their own baby's shawl, wrapped round a cushion – and had stolen the dog quite easily when the judging of the Alsatians was going on. They wrapped the tiny dog in the shawl, just as you thought, and caught the next train home!'

'I *wish* I'd gone to Seagreen Village with you,' said Julian. 'Do you know who told the couple to steal the little dog?'

'Yes – we're off to interview him now! He'll be very surprised to see us,' said the burly policeman. 'We've informed the owner that we've got her prize dog all right – but she feels so upset about it she can't collect it till the morning – so we

...ondered if you'd like to keep it for the night? Your Timmy can guard it, can't he?'

'Oh *yes*,' said George in delight. 'Oh, Mum – I'll take it to my room when I go to bed, and Timmy can guard the tiny thing as much as he likes. He'll love it!'

'Well – if your mum doesn't mind you having *two* dogs in your room, that's fine!' said the policeman, and signalled to the second one to give George the dog in the shawl. She took it gently, and Timmy leapt up again.

'No, Tim – be careful,' said George. 'Look what a tiny thing it is. You're to guard it tonight.'

Timmy looked at the little sleeping Pekinese, and then, very gently, he licked it with the tip of his pink tongue. This was the tiny dog he had smelt in the train, covered up in the shawl. Oh yes – Timmy had guessed at once!

'I don't know what your name is,' said Dick, stroking the small silky head. 'But I *think* I'll call you Half-term Adventure, although I don't know what that is in Pekinese!'

The two policemen laughed. 'Well, goodnight, everyone,' said the burly one. 'Mrs Fulton, the dog's owner, will call tomorrow morning for her Peke. He won a thousand-pound prize today – so I expect you'll get some of that for a reward! Goodnight!'

The Five didn't want a reward, of course – but Timmy had one for guarding the little Peke all night. It's on his neck – the finest studded collar he has ever had in his life! Good old Timmy!

7 *Happy Christmas, Five!*

Christmas Eve at Kirrin Cottage – and the Five
were all there together! They were up in the boys'
bedroom, wrapping Christmas presents in bright
paper. Timmy was very excited, and nosed about
the room, his long tail wagging in delight.

'Don't keep slapping my legs with your tail,
Tim,' said Anne. 'Look out, George, he's getting
tangled up with your ball of string!'

'Don't look round, Anne, I'm wrapping up
your present,' said Dick. 'There'll be a lot to give
out this Christmas, with all of us here – and
everyone giving everyone else something!'

'I've a B-O-N-E for Timmy,' said Anne, 'but it's
downstairs in the larder. I was afraid he'd sniff it
out up here.'

'Woof,' said Timmy, slapping his tail against
Anne's legs again.

'He knows perfectly well that B-O-N-E spells
bone,' said Julian. 'Now you've made him

sniff all about *my* parcels! Timmy – go downstairs, please!'

'Oh no – he does so love Christmas time, and helping us to wrap up parcels,' said George. 'Sit, Timmy. SIT, I say. That's the third time you've knocked down my pile of presents.'

Downstairs, her father and mother were wrapping up parcels, too. They seemed to have as many the four cousins upstairs! Mrs Kirrin looked at the pile of packages on the table.

'Far too many to go on the tree!' she said. 'We'd better put all our parcels and the children's too into a sack, Quentin. We can stand the sack at the bottom of the tree, and you can be Father Christmas and hand them out tomorrow morning.'

'I am NOT going to be Father Christmas,' said Mr Kirrin. 'All this nonsense at Christmas time! Bits of paper everywhere – parcels to undo – Timmy barking his head off. Listen to him now! I'll go mad! He's to go to his kennel.'

'No, no, Quentin – don't upset George on Christmas Eve,' said Mrs Kirrin. 'Look – you go and sit down quietly in your study and read the paper. *I'll* finish the parcels. But you MUST be good and hand them out to the children tomorrow morning – yes, and hand Timmy's to him too.'

Supper-time came all too soon that night. When the bell rang to tell the Five that the meal was ready, they groaned.

'Have to finish afterwards,' said Dick, looking round at the mess of parcels, paper, string, ribbon and labels. 'Supper, Timmy, supper!'

Timmy shot downstairs at top speed, bumping heavily into Mr Kirrin, who was just coming out of his study. Timmy gave him a quick lick of apology, and ran into the dining room, putting his front feet on the table to see what was there.

'Down, Timmy – what manners!' said Julian. 'Hello, Uncle Quentin – done up all your parcels yet?'

His uncle grunted. Aunt Fanny laughed. 'He's going to be Father Christmas tomorrow morning and hand out all the presents,' she said. 'Don't scowl like that, Quentin dear – you look just like George when I tell her to fetch something!'

'I do NOT scowl,' said George, scowling immediately, of course. Everyone roared at her, and she had to smile.

'Christmas Day tomorrow,' said Anne happily.

'Aunt Fanny, it's lovely of you to have us all here for Christmas. We'll never finish opening our parcels tomorrow morning! I've got at least one for everybody, and so has everyone else.'

'A nice little bit of arithmetic,' said Julian. 'That means we've about forty or more presents to undo – counting in those for Joanna and Timmy.'

'What a waste of time!' That remark came from Uncle Quentin, of course!

'It's a good thing you're not as horrible as you pretend to be, Dad,' said George, and grinned at him. 'You always look so fierce – and yet I bet you've been round the shops buying all kinds of things. Hasn't he, Mum? I bet he's bought Timmy something, too.'

'Stop saying "I bet",' said her father. 'And don't put ideas in Timmy's head. Why on earth should I go shopping for *him*?'

'Woof!' said Timmy, from under the table, delighted to hear his name. He wagged his tail violently and Mr Kirrin leapt to his feet with a yell.

'Take that dog out! Slapping me with his tail like that! Why can't he have a short tail? I'll . . .'

'Sit down, Quentin,' said his wife. 'Timmy,

come out. Sit over there. Now – let's change the subject!'

The four cousins looked at one another and grinned. It *was* lovely to be at Kirrin Cottage again, with dear kind Aunt Fanny, and quick-tempered Uncle Quentin. He was now beaming round at them, offering them a second helping.

'No thanks,' said Dick. 'I'm saving up for the pudding. I spotted it in the larder – scrumptious!'

After supper they finished their parcels, and brought them all down to the sitting room. The tree was there, looking very cheerful, although the candles on it were not yet lighted. It was hung with tinsel and little sparkling ornaments, and had at the top the fairy doll that had been on every Christmas tree since George was little.

The parcels were put into a big sack, and this was set at the foot of the tree, ready for the morning. Timmy immediately went to sniff at it, from top to bottom.

'He can smell his Christmas bone,' said Anne. 'Timmy, come away. I won't have you guessing my present!'

Later they played games, and Timmy joined in.

He was so excited that he began to bark, and Uncle Quentin stormed out of his study at once, and appeared in the sitting room.

'George! I've told you before I won't have Timmy barking in the house. Yes, I know it's Christmas Eve, but I can't STAND that barking. Why must he have such a loud one? It's enough to deafen me. I'll turn him out. He can go to his kennel!'

'Oh *no*, Dad – not on Christmas Eve!' said George, horrified. 'Timmy, go and lie down – and BE QUIET!'

'He's to go out to his kennel,' said her father. 'That's my last word. Out, Timmy, OUT!'

So out poor Timmy had to go, his tail well down. He felt puzzled. The children had been shouting, hadn't they? It was their way of barking. Well, why couldn't *he* shout in *his* own way, which was barking?

George was cross, and Anne was almost in tears. Poor Timmy – to be sent out to his kennel on Christmas Eve! She went to comfort George, and was surprised to see that she wasn't looking upset.

'Don't worry, Anne – I'll fetch him in when we

go to bed and he can sleep in our room as usual,' she said.

'You can't do that!' said Anne. 'Uncle Quentin would be *furious* if he discovered him there.'

'He won't,' said George. 'It's no good, Anne – I'm going to have Timmy with me tonight, although I KNOW I shouldn't. I couldn't bear not to. I'll own up to Dad tomorrow.'

So, when the household was safely in bed, George crept downstairs to fetch Timmy from his kennel. He whined softly in joy and wagged his big tail.

'Be quiet now,' whispered George, and took him upstairs – completely forgetting to lock the kitchen door! Timmy settled down on the rug beside her bed, very happy, and soon Anne and George were fast asleep in their beds, while the two boys slept soundly in their room nearby.

All four were awakened by a terrific bout of barking from Timmy! He stood at the bedroom door, scraping at it, trying to open it, barking at the top of his voice! George leapt out of bed in alarm.

'What is it, Timmy? What is it? Stop barking – Dad'll hear you and know you're in the house and not in your kennel. Oh DO shut up, Timmy!'

But by this time everyone was wide awake, and soon the whole household was out on the landing, alarmed. George's father was very angry when he saw that Timmy was in the house after all. 'Why isn't he in his kennel? What's the matter with him? How DARE you disobey me, George?'

'Take him out to his kennel at once, George,' said her mother, very cross too. 'He's over-excited tonight – it was all that fun and games you had. Take him out at once.'

'But, Mum – he doesn't usually bark. Perhaps there was a burglar in the house,' said poor George.

'Nonsense!' said her father, angrily. 'No burglar would come on Christmas Eve. Take the dog out to his kennel – and don't let me hear another sound tonight!'

'Go on, George, now,' said her mother. 'Do as you're told and don't spoil Christmas.'

Timmy was very sad to be put into his kennel again. He whined dismally, and George almost made up her mind to stay outside with him. But his kennel wasn't big enough to take both of them, so she gave him a hug and went indoors with Anne, scowling in the darkness. This time she remembered to lock the door behind her! Soon everyone was in bed again, and sound asleep.

Anne awoke a little while later and sat up in bed. She had heard something – some noise downstairs. She sat and listened. *Was* there someone in the sitting room? Then she heard a click. 'Like a door being shut,' she thought, and wondered if she should wake George. No – surely Timmy would bark loudly if *he* heard anything suspicious – he was only just outside, in his kennel. Perhaps he *had* heard something when he had barked before.

'Well, anyway, I'm not going downstairs by myself in the dark,' thought Anne. 'And I really daren't wake Uncle or Aunt. I must leave Timmy to deal with whatever it is. He can always bark or howl if someone is about!'

Timmy *had* heard something, and he was sitting in his kennel, ears pricked up, a little growl grumbling in his throat. He really didn't dare to bark this time. He had heard something before, when he had barked in George's bedroom, and awakened the whole household – and yet there had been nobody downstairs then that he could see or smell!

But somebody *was* in the house – someone who had crept in at the kitchen door, when George had left it unlocked! That Somebody had hidden in the coal cellar, door fast shut, when Timmy had barked and alarmed the household! Now the Somebody was about again, switching on a small torch, making the little noises that had awakened Anne.

It was Tom, the bad boy of the village! He had been out to a rowdy party, and had passed Kirrin Cottage on his way home. He had tiptoed to the front door, and gone to the garden door and tried both handles – no, they were locked! Then he had slipped round to the kitchen door, and to his surprise and delight had found it opened when he turned the handle.

He had crept inside and was just looking round when Timmy had begun to bark upstairs – and quick as a rabbit Tom had slipped into the coal cellar, and shivered there while the household came out on to the landing, angry with Timmy, who was then put into his kennel.

When all was quiet, and the dog safely in his kennel, the boy looked quietly round to see what he could take. He thought he heard a noise, and stopped in alarm. No, it was only the coals dropping in the grate. He felt scared, and swung his torch round and about to see what he could easily take away with him.

He saw the sack lying by the Christmas tree – how it bulged with the parcels inside it! Tom grinned in delight. 'Must be full of wonderful presents!' he thought. 'All nicely bundled up in a sack, too – couldn't be easier for me to carry!'

He lifted it, put it over his shoulder, and tiptoed out of the kitchen door, shutting it with a little click – the click that Anne had heard from upstairs!

Timmy knew there was someone about, of course – but now he didn't dare to bark. He had been put into his kennel as a punishment for barking – if he barked again and woke Mr Kirrin, goodness knows what would happen to him! So he kept completely silent, and slipped out of his kennel, and down the garden path after the boy with the sack.

He followed him all the way to the village,

unseen and unheard. How he longed to growl, how he longed to fly at this nasty little robber-boy and nip him sharply in the leg! He saw the boy go through a gate and walk to a shed nearby. He went in, and came out again – but this time without the sack! Then he let himself into the house nearby, shut the door, and disappeared.

Timmy sat down to think. After a minute he went to the shed and slipped through the half-broken wooden door. He smelt the sack at once. That bulging sack belonged to George! Very well – it must at once be taken back to Kirrin Cottage before the boy took out all the presents in it. Timmy sniffed at the parcels inside. His own parcel was there – the one with the bone that Anne had wrapped up for him. Timmy growled. So that boy had DARED to carry away his bone! Timmy decided to take the whole sack back to Kirrin Cottage.

But it was far too heavy for him to drag out of the shed! What was he to do? He worked his head into the open sack neck again and pulled out a parcel – then another and another! Good – he would take them one by one to his kennel and hide them there for Christmas morning!

And that is exactly what dear, patient Timmy did! He took all those parcels one by one to his kennel, trotting back and forth so many times that he began to feel he was walking in a dream! It was lucky that Kirrin Cottage wasn't far from the boy's home, or he would have been trotting to and fro all night!

At last the sack was empty, and the last parcel safely tucked into the back of his big kennel. There was hardly room for Timmy to sit in it! Tired out but very happy, he put down his head on his paws, and fell sound asleep.

He was awakened next morning by a great hubbub in Kirrin Cottage! 'Aunt Fanny! Uncle Quentin! The sack of presents is gone – and the kitchen door's wide open! Someone's stolen all our presents in the night.'

'That's why Timmy barked! He *knew* there was something going on! Oh, our beautiful presents! What a MEAN trick!'

'But why didn't Tim catch the thief when he slipped out of the kitchen door with the sack? Poor Tim – he must have been too scared to do anything, after being scolded for barking before, and made to go to his kennel!'

'Christmas is spoilt!' said Anne, with tears in her eyes. 'No presents at all – no surprises – no fun!'

'Woof!' said Timmy, coming out of his kennel, as the four children came up the path. 'Woof!'

'Who took our lovely presents, Timmy – and where do you think they are now?' said George, sorrowfully. 'Didn't you dare to bark?'

'Woof,' said Timmy, in an apologetic voice, and went into his kennel. He backed out with something in his mouth – a parcel! He went in and fetched another – and another – and another! He laid them all down in front of the astounded children, wagging his tail.

'TIMMY! Where did you get them? Where's the sack? Did you chase the thief, and take the parcels one by one out of the sack – and bring them home?' asked George, in wonder.

'Woof,' said Timmy, agreeing, and wagged his tail vigorously. He pawed at one of the parcels, and Anne gave a delighted laugh.

'That's *my* present to *you*!' she said. 'You *knew* it was for you, Tim – you smelt the bone inside. Darling, darling Tim, how clever you are! You stored all our presents safely in your kennel, so that we'd have them on Christmas morning after all! I'll undo your parcel and you'll have *my* present first of all!'

'WOOF, WOOF, WOOF!' barked Timmy, in delight, and not even Uncle Quentin frowned at the tremendous noise.

'Good old Timmy! Open your parcel and then go indoors and gnaw your bone, while you watch the others open theirs.'

Happy Christmas to all the Five – and especially to you, Timmy-dog, especially to you!

8 When Timmy chased the cat!

'What are you going to do today?' said Aunt Fanny to the Five.

They all looked up from their books – except Timmy, who looked up from the bone he was gnawing.

'We ought to go for a walk, I suppose,' said Julian. 'But the wind's so bitter today. I always think January is a pretty dreary month, unless there's snow – or we can go skating.'

'But there's no snow, and no ice – only this horrible, freezing wind,' said Anne. 'I'd just as soon stay in and read my Christmas books!'

'Oh no – we *must* go out,' said George at once. 'What about Timmy? He's got to have his usual walk.'

Timmy's ears pricked up at once when he heard that word. Walk! Ha – just what he was wanting! He got up at once and ran to George, whining. She patted him.

'All right, all right, Tim – we'll leave Anne here with her books, and we'll go out for a nice long walk.'

'Would you like to go to the cinema in Beckton?' asked her mother. 'There's a good film on today, about circus life. I'll pay for you all, if you'd like to go this afternoon.'

'Mum – I think you're trying to get rid of us!' said George.

'Well – in a way I am,' said her mother, with a laugh. 'Your dad has two friends coming to see him this afternoon – and I really think it would be easier if you were out of the house.'

'Oh, I *see*,' said George. 'Two more of his scientist friends, I suppose. Well, I'd just as soon be out in that case. It's awful not even to be able to sneeze in case I get into trouble for making a noise.'

'Don't exaggerate, George,' said her mother. 'Well, Julian – would *you* like to go to the cinema?'

'Of course – and it's very kind of you to pay for us,' said Julian. 'I tell you what – we'll *walk* to Beckton, so that we'll give our legs a stretch – and get the train back.'

'Yes. That's a good idea,' said Dick. 'I feel as if I want a good run. Just listen to Tim thumping his tail on the ground. He thoroughly agrees!'

So that afternoon, the Five set off to walk to Beckton. The wind was in their faces, and it was very cold indeed; but they were soon warm with walking, and even Anne began to enjoy striding out against the wind.

Timmy loved it, of course. He was full of high spirits, and pranced and capered and bounded about joyfully. He wagged his long tail nineteen to the dozen, chased dead leaves as if they were rats, and made everyone laugh at him.

'Dear Tim,' said Anne. 'It must be lovely to be a dog, and have four legs to leap about on, instead of just two!'

Halfway to Beckton they came to a big, rather lonely-looking house called Tarleys Mount. The gates opened on to a short drive that ran to the front steps of the house. On the top of one of the stone gateposts sat a big black cat. It looked disdainfully down at Timmy.

At first Timmy didn't see it, and then he suddenly caught sight of it and stopped. A cat! And a big one, too. But sadly, just out of reach!

Timmy pranced in front of the gatepost and barked loudly. The cat yawned widely, and then began to wash one of her paws, as if to say – 'A dog! Nasty smelly creature! Not worth taking notice of!'

But Timmy could leap very high, and the cat was suddenly startled to see his head appearing near the top of the gatepost as he jumped. She hissed and spat.

'Stop it, Timmy,' said George. 'You know you're not allowed to chase cats. Come here!'

The cat spat again. That was too much for Timmy, and he jumped so high that the cat was really alarmed. She leapt right off the gatepost, and shot into the bushes at the side of the drive.

Timmy was after her in a flash, yelping madly. George yelled, but he took no notice at all.

'Bad dog,' said Julian. 'He'll be ages chasing that cat and hunting for it. He ought to know by now that he isn't a match for any cat living!'

'I'll go in and see if I can get him,' said George. 'Hope I don't meet an angry gardener!'

'We'll come with you,' said Dick. 'Come on. I can hear Tim down the drive. He must be near the house.'

They went in at the gate and down the little drive. Yes – Timmy was by the front door, barking under a tree there.

'I bet the cat's sitting on a branch making faces at him,' said Julian. 'Call him, George.'

'Timmy, Timmy! Come here at once!' shouted George. But he wouldn't. Then just as they got up to him and George was bending down to take hold of his collar, the cat leapt down the tree and raced round the house to the back. Timmy was after her at once, yelping madly.

'Oh *no*! said George, vexed. 'We'll have the people of the house out after us – they must wonder what's going on!'

They ran round the house after Timmy, and came to the back entrance. There was a little yard there, with a clothes line and two or three dustbins and a coal bunker. The cat was now sitting on top of the bunker, daring Timmy to leap up and get her.

'Now then, you dog – you leave that cat alone!' said an angry voice as the four children turned into the yard. They saw a neat little woman standing there, in a thick coat with a scarf round her head. She held a small basket in her hand, with a little bottle of milk in it and a jar.

'I'm so sorry about our dog,' said George, and pounced on Timmy. She got hold of his collar this time and spoke to him sharply. 'I'm ashamed of you! Bad dog! Very bad dog.'

Timmy's tail drooped, and he gave George's hand a very small lick. The little woman watched him, frowning.

'He gave me a real fright, that dog of yours,' she said. 'Tearing into the yard like a mad thing – first old Sooty the cat – then the dog!'

'I hope his barking didn't disturb the people in the house,' said Julian.

'What's that you say?' said the woman, cupping her hand behind her ear. 'I'm a bit deaf.'

'I said, I hope his barking didn't disturb the people in the house!' repeated Julian in a louder voice.

'Oh, they're away,' said the little woman, taking off the top of the milk bottle. 'Miss Ella went on Monday, and her old aunt went yesterday. I just came to feed the old cat. Here, Sooty – come and lap your milk, and I'll put your fish down, too. Hold that dog, please.'

She emptied some cooked fish out of the jar,

and poured milk into an enamel saucer by the back doorstep. The cat sat on the coal bunker and looked down longingly, but wouldn't come near it.

'We'll take the dog and go,' said Dick.

'What did you say?' said the woman. 'Oh yes – you go; then old Sooty will come along down. He must be hungry.'

The four children went round the house again, George holding Timmy's collar.

'Funny – I can hear somebody talking!' said Anne, suddenly, as they went along the drive. 'Can you, Dick?'

'Yes,' said Dick, puzzled. 'But there's nobody about.'

They all stopped to listen.

'It sounds like a loud conversation,' said Julian. 'Is it coming from the house?'

'No – you heard what the woman said. The people are away,' said George. 'It must be somebody talking very loudly in the road.'

But the talking couldn't be heard when they reached the gates. 'Oh well – it was probably gardeners somewhere in the trees off the drive,' said Dick. 'Come on – we'll be late for the film, if we don't hurry up.'

They were just in time for it and settled down to watch the circus story on the screen. It was very good, and they all enjoyed it thoroughly. They collected Timmy from the kindly attendant, and he barked in welcome. They felt very hungry, and the little café opposite looked very inviting, with its wonderful display of cakes in the window.

'Come on – I'll buy tea for everyone – providing George doesn't eat more than six cakes!' said Julian, rattling the money in his pocket. 'Timmy, I'll buy you one too.'

They had a wonderful tea, and finished up with an ice-cream each. Timmy was treated to a cake and a biscuit, and licked George's ice-cream saucer clean.

'Well – I don't know if we can *manage* to walk to the station now!' said Dick. 'I feel pretty full. What's the matter, George?'

'I was just feeling Timmy's collar – and he's lost his Tail Wagger badge,' said George. 'It's got his name and address on it. Oh no! I only bought him a new one last week.'

'If we want to catch the train back, we'd better

get a move on,' said Julian, looking at his watch.

'No, I'm going to walk home,' said George. 'I've got a torch. I may find Timmy's badge.'

'Oh, for pity's sake!' groaned Dick. 'Don't say we've got to walk back hunting for the badge all the way home. No, George – that's too much.'

'I can go alone, with Timmy,' said George. 'I didn't mean you others to come.'

'Well – we can't let you walk a mile or two home in the dark by yourself,' said Julian. 'I tell you what – I'll go with *you*, George, and Dick and Anne can go back by train.'

'No, thanks,' said Anne. 'I'll come too. I think *I* know where Tim dropped his badge. In the drive of that big house! Do you remember when the cat sat up in a tree and Timmy leapt up at her? Well, he caught his collar on a bough – and I bet that's when he lost his Tail Wagger badge.'

'Yes – I expect you're right,' said George. 'Timmy's being a bit of a nuisance today – aren't you, Tim? I hope that cat won't be anywhere about in the garden.'

'Tie a bit of string to Tim's collar,' said Dick, producing a piece. 'And hang on to him, George! Well – are we ready?'

They all set off in the starry night. They hardly needed their torches once they had got used to the dark, because the stars were so very bright. They came at last to Tarleys Mount, and stopped at the gates.

'Here we are,' said Dick, flashing his torch. 'We know where Timmy went this morning, and if we hunt about we're pretty certain to find the badge.'

'Now, you keep by me, Tim,' said George, holding tightly to the string lead.

They all went down the drive – and in the middle of it they stopped in surprise.

'I can hear those voices *again* – well, different ones this time – but *voices*!' said Anne, astonished. 'Who can be out here, talking and talking in the night?'

'Beats me!' said Dick. 'Come on – let's go to that tree by the front door. I bet the badge will be there!'

They went to the big door, still hearing the voices somewhere away in the distance. Anne suddenly gave a cry, and bent down. 'Yes – here's the badge, just where I thought it might be. Isn't that lucky?'

'Oh good!' said George, and fixed it on Timmy's collar.

'There's somebody *singing* now,' said Dick, standing still and listening. 'It's really odd.'

'Perhaps it's a radio somewhere,' said Anne. 'It sounds a bit like one.'

'But there's no other house near here,' said Julian. 'Not near enough for us to hear the radio, anyway.'

The singing voice stopped – and band music came on the air. 'There!' said Anne. 'That's the radio all right! There can't be any band playing in the open air this cold night.'

'You're right,' said Julian, puzzled. 'Do you think that the sounds can be coming from *this* house – Tarleys Mount?'

'But we know there's no one *there*,' said Dick. 'That woman who fed the cat this morning told us the house was empty. That's why she had to come and feed the cat. And if someone had left the radio on in the house, she'd have heard it and switched it off.'

'No, she wouldn't,' said George.

'Why not?' asked Dick, surprised.

'Well, because she was *deaf*!' said George. 'She

kept putting her hand behind her ear, don't you remember? *I* think the radio *is* on in the house.'

'You don't think somebody's got in, and is having a good time there – eating what's left in the larder, sleeping in the beds, and listening to the radio, do you?' said Anne. 'Tramps – or gipsies perhaps.'

'It's a bit puzzling,' said Julian. 'I can't imagine anyone going away and leaving the radio *full* on – and it must be, if we can hear it out here. Perhaps we ought to look round a bit. The noise seems to come from over there – the other side of the house, not where the yard is. Let's go round there.'

There was a sudden hiss from a nearby bush, and Timmy pricked up his ears. That cat again!

'Hang on to Tim – there's the cat,' said Julian, as a black streak fled across the beam of his torch. 'Come on, now – let's go round the other side of the house.'

As soon as they turned the corner, they came to a terrace, with steps leading down to a garden only faintly to be seen in the starlight. The band music was suddenly louder there. There was now no doubt at all that it was radio music.

'Well – it's certainly coming from the house,'

said Julian. 'But from which room? As far as I can see, the whole place is in darkness!'

So it was! Not a chink of light showed anywhere. Julian shone his torch on to each window. They were all tightly shut, as if the house were indeed empty and deserted.

'There's a tree that reaches up to that balcony,' said Dick. 'I'll shin up and get on to it, and see if I can spot anything in the house. If the curtains aren't drawn there, I can shine my torch in.'

Up the tree he went, the others shining their torches to show him which branches to climb. At last he was on the balcony, his own torch now shining brightly. There were glass doors there, and the curtains of the room behind weren't drawn across the panes. Dick shone his torch through the glass.

'The radio's in this room, I'm sure!' he cried. 'I can hear it clearly. It's on full, too – the noise is coming through a ventilator, above the glass doors! Oh!'

'What? What is it?' cried everyone, hearing a sudden strange note in Dick's excited voice.

'There's someone in this room!' called back Dick. 'Someone lying on the floor, but I can't see clearly enough. Whoever it is isn't moving at all. I'll tap and see if they hear me.'

The others heard the sound of tapping, and then Dick's voice again. 'Yes – the person moved when I tapped. Who on earth can it be? He must be hurt, I think but the doors are locked, so I can't get in. I'm coming down again, so shine your torches, will you?'

Dick climbed quickly down the tree, and the others crowded round him excitedly. 'We'll have to get into the house somehow,' said Dick. 'I'm sure it's someone who's hurt – or maybe ill.'

'But how did they get in?' said Julian in wonder. 'And how can we get in, for that matter?'

'We'll try all the doors to begin with,' said Dick. 'Here's a garden door. No, that's locked. Come on round to the kitchen door. I suppose that'll be locked, too.'

But it wasn't! It opened easily enough, and the Five trooped into the house, Timmy quite excited. The noise of the radio suddenly seemed much louder as they went in.

'Come on upstairs,' said Dick. 'We'll find that balcony room. It was all in darkness, which made it seem stranger than ever!'

They ran up the wide stairs. The sound of the radio was very loud there. They listened intently. 'It's in that room over there!' shouted Dick, and ran to a half-open door. He shone his torch round, and then let the beam rest on something lying on the floor. What could it be?

Julian reached out his hand to the light switch by the door. Click! The light flooded the room and everyone blinked. The radio went on and on all the time, the dance band playing away gaily.

On the floor near the radio lay a woman. She looked old and had silvery grey hair. She was dressed in outdoor things, and her hat lay on the floor.

The children looked at her in horror – what *could* have happened? At last, to their relief, they saw her eyes open, and she looked up at them. Then she tried to speak.

'Water!' she croaked.

George darted out and found a bathroom with glasses. She filled one with water and brought it back. Julian eased the old woman up into a sitting position, and George helped her to drink the water. She managed to give them a faint smile.

'So silly of me,' she said, in a faraway kind of

voice. 'I was just going downstairs to leave the house by the back door, when I slipped here on the polished floor. And, and—'

She stopped for a moment, and Anne patted her hand. 'You fell and hurt yourself?' she said. 'Where?'

'I'm afraid it's my hip,' said the old lady. 'I couldn't get up off the floor. I just couldn't. So I wasn't even able to phone for help. And there was no one in the house – my niece had gone—'

'And your daily woman is deaf, so she wouldn't hear you call!' said Julian, remembering.

'Yes, yes,' said the old lady. 'I just managed to get my arm up to the radio and switched it on. You see, I thought *someone* might hear it – perhaps a policeman coming round the house at night . . .'

'How long have you been lying like this?' asked Anne anxiously.

'Since yesterday afternoon,' said the old lady. 'I *just* couldn't move, you see. I *was* glad I had my outdoor things on – I'd have frozen stiff last night, it was so cold! I was so thirsty, too. Not hungry. Just very, very thirsty. You dear, kind children – oh, I *am* so glad to see you!'

Julian switched off the radio. 'Where's the phone?' he said. 'I'll call for a doctor – and an ambulance – and you'll soon be well cared for! Don't you worry!'

The Five stayed with her until the doctor came and, later on, the ambulance. Then Julian turned out all the lights that had been switched on, and they went into the hall. Julian slammed the front door after them.

'Come on, Timmy – keep by my side,' ordered George. 'No more cat-chasing for you!'

'What's he saying, George?' asked Anne.

George chuckled. 'He says, "Don't talk to me like that, George – if it hadn't been for me chasing that cat today, you'd never have had this little adventure".'

'Well, Timmy's right, as usual,' said Dick. 'And if chasing a cat leads to saving somebody's life, I'm all for it. Good old Tim!'

Enid Blyton™

THE
FAMOUS FIVE'S
SURVIVAL GUIDE

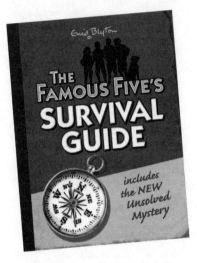

Packed with useful information on surviving outdoors and solving mysteries, here is the one mystery that the Famous Five never managed to solve. See if you can follow the trail to discover the location of the priceless Royal Dragon of Siam.

The perfect book for all fans of mystery, adventure and the Famous Five!

ISBN 9780340970836

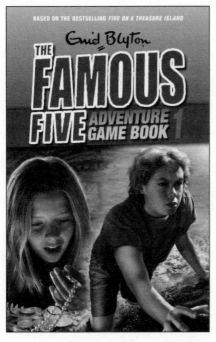